A Dash of

Death

A Southern Fried Cozy Mystery

Jamie Lee Scott

A DASH OF DEATH

This morning, I had a photo shoot for a new coffee shop in Irving, TX who wanted a new and fun look for their posters and POP (point of purchase) materials. Something that reflected their industrial stores, but with a hint of "relaxed." Phffffft, there was nothing relaxing about coffee or the coffee business. It was craziness, with crazy customers. Crazy dedicated customers, that is. Fast food was probably the only other food service business that had customers come in every day of the week. Or close to it. And I wanted my coffee photos to help make this Irving coffee business thrive.

I'd already practiced with my first latte, and was headed to the sink to dump it out when there was a knock on the door. Oliver, my black and white Border Collie, growled, then let out a deep bark. He sounded so mean and looked mean too as the hair on his back stood up. I sat the white porcelain cup on the counter next to the sink and walked over to unlock the door.

My studio was in a cottage a few doors from my home, both of which belonged to my mother-in-law. I had signed a ten-year lease for the studio right before I divorced her son, which was two years ago. I'd say I was stuck, but I really liked the location. And I loved not having to drive to work.

Hettie Savoie, the matriarch of Savoie Inc., treated me like a daughter. A red-headed stepchild of a daughter, but daughter all the same. Her son owned and ran Savoie's restaurant, and she treated him like the salt of the earth, except when he made her mad.

Savoie is a French Creole name, and Hettie was proud of her and her husband's heritage. When they finally married and settled in Texas, they kept their Creole heritage intact, when it was convenient. I thought the name Savoie sounded chic. Too bad no one could pronounce it properly unless they spoke French. The family didn't much care if people could pronounce the name, so long as they came to their businesses to eat and drink. The property housed a vineyard, winery, bed and breakfast with a bistro called Le Bon Gout, and Pierre's fine dining restaurant, Savoie. It was also home to Hettie Savoie, whose expansive ranch house overlooked it all. We stayed in one of the old workers' houses up the hill a little way from the bed and breakfast. Hettie had completely remodeled into an elegant home as a wedding gift.

Most of the time when I was working, I kept the door to my work studio locked. I didn't like to be bothered when I was working, and Hettie and my ex-husband, Pierre, loved to walk in quietly to try to scare the crap out of me. Since they both lived and worked on the property, they seemed to always be around. Not only did I not like their intrusions, but they'd also inevitably catch me on a tedious project, and I'd end up spending at least an hour fixing what got messed up when I jumped. Or I'd have to start from the beginning in some cases. Such a waste of time and money.

"Home," I said to Oliver, before I opened the front door. Oliver tucked his tail between his legs and walked as slow as he could to his crate. Oliver loved his crate and spent most of the time while I worked laying inside with his head hanging out on the floor.

Jared Guidry stood in the doorway, looking adorable in his chef's pants and white coat. I fully expected him to pull out a toque and put it on his head after he walked in. The young sous chef, I guessed him to be about twenty-five, would've had the girls in Savoie Restaurant all a flutter with his dirty blonde hair and big brown eyes. Luckily, he wouldn't be working in the restaurant or the winery. He was all mine. His wide grin, not quite perfect teeth, and dimples made him look a lot younger. And sort of made me with I was younger. Then I mentally slapped that thought right out of my head.

"Hey, I thought maybe I was early," he said. "The door being locked and all."

I looked at my watch. "Actually, you're thirty minutes late."

He pulled his phone from his pocket. "Oh, man, I'm so sorry. I was listening to music in my car and fell asleep. I had a late night last night."

What I wouldn't give for a late night that wasn't work related. I patted him on the shoulder. "Last time this will happen, right? I need you to be punctual. What if our client had been here for the styling and photo shoot?"

He shrugged.

I took this as his understanding that he wouldn't have a job if he was late again, but I didn't push it because it wasn't really that big of a deal. Not at the time anyway.

"We're starting with a photo shoot for a coffeehouse this morning. Then this afternoon, we'll be working on a pasta dish for my blog. I'll be teaching you some of my styling techniques."

"I'm a pasta master," he said, heading over to the hand washing sink to wash his hands. "Where're the gloves?"

"Gloves?" I asked.

"Yeah, food service gloves." He looked at me like it was *my* first day on the job.

At this point Oliver let it be known that he was the man of the studio by offering a long growl.

Jared's eyes widened as he looked for the source of the sound.

"Don't worry, he's more afraid of you than you are of him. He's only dangerous to livestock."

"You have a dog in here? Isn't that against state regulations?"

Ha, he had a lot to learn. "We aren't serving this food to the public. In fact, most of it will never be eaten. At least not on purpose. No gloves needed, unless we're working with food dye, and don't want to get your fingers stained. And I've never had a dog hair in any of my photos. Now, if we're testing a recipe we plan to eat, that's a different story. We wear gloves, and the dog stays out of the kitchen."

Jared jerked his chin toward the dog crate. "Does it have a name?"

"His name is Oliver. He'll be friendly enough once he gets to know you."

"Cool." He looked at the latte on the counter. "This looks good. You have an espresso machine?"

"That is our project for the morning." I pointed to the coffee machine. "I do have an old-fashioned coffee maker if you want to start a pot. I only keep decaf in the studio, so I don't get the shakes from the caffeine."

Jared dried his hands, then walked over to my prep table. I saw his hands shaking already; he didn't need any caffeine. "That coffee looked delicious. This is going to be fun, I think."

I sure hoped he liked it. Training a new assistant was a pain in the butt. Teaching all the trade secrets, and the tedious ins and outs of food styling took time and money. I really disliked training because it took me longer to get my job done. But once he had a good handle, my job would be so much easier, and I could concentrate more on the photography and my blog. I hoped his sous chef experience would mean he'd be on his own quickly.

"The key is attention to detail on the front end, which is the production side. The camera sees everything and magnifies every flaw. I prefer to get it right in production, so I don't have to do so much retouching work in post-production."

Earlier that morning, I'd placed four white coffee cups on a bar towel on the concrete countertop of my studio kitchen prep area, along with a bottle of clear dishwashing detergent, a bottle of soy sauce, and some clear foaming hand soap.

Before I could even show Jared how to make the "coffee," I heard the door to my studio open. Damn, I'd forgotten to relock when I let Jared in. It opened slowly and quietly, as the perpetrator was hoping I had my earbuds in, or I was engrossed in a tedious project. I put my finger up to my lips and turned to watch my mother-in-law creep into the room.

"Good morning, Hettie." I leaned against the counter and smiled.

She looked up, clearly disappointed. Acting innocent, as if she hadn't planned to scare the crap out of me, she asked, "Did you get a new car?"

Even though Hettie was a savvy businesswoman, she could be so immature. I never worked for her, but living on her property made me an easy target.

Hettie not only ran her own conglomerate, which included partnering with Pierre and I on the Savoie, she also owned the winery, vineyards, bed and breakfast, and the bistro, she also headed up several foundations. Her name had become synonymous with Piney Woods, which is a nickname for the beautiful landscape of East Texas. The way she looked this morning, no one would mistake her for a savvy businesswoman.

She wore neon pink Lycra running pants and black running shoes with a pink swoosh. Her razor back, skintight top belonged on a twenty-year-old, not a seventy-year-old, but I had to give her credit, she wore it well. Being five-four and weighing maybe a hundred pounds, she took her running seriously, and it showed.

"No, why?"

"I saw a strange car in front of the cottage. Where's your car?"

"Pierre has it."

"Whatever for? He has his Mercedes. Why would he drive your old jalopy?"

What she meant by jalopy was my two-year-old Lexus.

"Isn't it a little chilly to be running without a jacket?" I asked, changing the subject.

Hettie patted her butt. "This little tush already ran ten miles today, so I'm perfectly fine. Cooling off now." She looked at Jared and I swear she winked. "Is this the owner of the car?"

"I guess it depends on what kind of car it is," he said. "I drive a Toyota Corolla. Dull gray."

Hettie sauntered up to Jared. "I'm Hettie Savoie, and you are?"

"Hettie," I never did call her Mom, "this is Jared Guidry, my new assistant."

"You look familiar. Do you take the yoga class at Stretch Armstrong's?" She looked him up and down.

He shook his head, not able to answer before she lost interest.

She looked over her shoulder at me. "He looks like a keeper." She reached up and pulled the elastic band from the messy bun at the top of her silver hair and let it cascade down her shoulders and back, like a shampoo commercial. I had to admit, she had the most beautiful gray hair, and could easily be in a shampoo commercial.

I blushed, embarrassed more for Jared than for Hettie.

"Did you need something, or did you just want to make sure no one was robbing the place?" As much as I loved her, she had bad timing, and I didn't want to spend the morning chatting with her.

Jared had moved to the sink again and started a pot of coffee.

She looked at her Apple Watch with the larger screen that looked ginormous on her bony wrist. "I'm here to remind you that you have a meeting with Annabel this afternoon about the Wine Train benefit."

The Wine Train benefit started thirty years ago as a small gathering of the wives of the vineyard owners. It was a day of wine tasting and whining about how many vineyards were popping up, and how that was going to affect their millions. Now, it was an annual event that raised money for children's charities. People came from all over to taste Texas and Louisiana wines, and savor appetizers made by the best chefs in East Texas. Tickets sold out every year.

"I have it on my calendar. But if I don't get started on my photo shoot, I'll have to reschedule. I'm training Jared today, so it's going to take me twice as long to get my client's work finished. You know, the work that I get paid for. That I pay the rent with."

"What happened to your last assistant?" she asked, knowing the answer all too well.

I looked at the clock on the wall. "Yeah, I'll probably have to reschedule."

"Don't you dare reschedule! I'll never hear the end of it. She was in a mood this morning, and I don't want a phone call from her this afternoon, whining about how she has to work around *your* schedule. That never goes over well."

"Fine." I turned back to the counter to assemble the coffee for photos.

With that, Hettie gave a finger wave to Jared and slammed the door behind her as she left.

"Sorry about that," I said to Jared as I listened to the glass in the door rattle.

He grinned. Those dimples again. "She's a firecracker."

"Yes, she is."

"And she's pretty hot for a grandma."

Now I blushed for Hettie.

CHAPTER 2

A fast learner, probably from his time in Dallas restaurant kitchens, Jared diluted the soy sauce, then poured it into the coffee cup. We had four different coffees to prep: black, latte, mocha, and coffee with cream.

I let Jared start with the easy stuff. I figured if he messed them up, he could do the dishes, which was the only part of the job I hated.

I'd explained to him how to make the "coffee" and he laughed, then got started.

Adding a few drops of clear detergent to a small amount of the diluted soy sauce, he then stirred it to make bubbles. Next, he spooned the bubbly liquid into the not quite full coffee cup that I'd placed on a paper towel. Black coffee. There are always little bubbles in a cup of black coffee.

"What happened to your last assistant, if you don't mind me asking?"

"She went away to college." She happened to be my daughter, Celine Savoie. I didn't name her, Pierre did, but the name fit.

I moved my lighting into place and took a series of photographs, then we added props. The client specifically said he didn't want coffee beans in the shot. So, I had Jared cut several fresh strawberries and fan them out. I picked the hero, placing it next to the cup, which was now on a saucer with a cube of brown sugar next to it. We changed the location, took a few more pictures, then added linen napkins, biscotti, and lastly, I dribbled a few drops of coffee on the counter and took more pictures.

After the black coffee, I showed Jared how to make a latte, or cappuccino, by pumping the foaming hand soap into a shallow bowl, then spooning it on top of the "coffee" before adding a dash of cinnamon. Or no cinnamon, depending on the product.

"This is so cool." He took a sip of the decaf coffee he'd made earlier, admiring the fake coffee. "I can't believe this isn't real coffee."

I took his cup of real coffee and sat it next to the black "coffee" that we hadn't used for the shoot yet. "The diluted soy works great for tea, too. It holds up better for a photography session."

"That's amazing. It looks tastier than my real coffee."

"It's supposed to." I laughed.

He looked at the clock. "Wow, it's already noon? That was the easiest two-plus hours I've spent in a kitchen in ages."

I looked up at the clock, too.

When I turned back around, I saw a milk foam mustache on Jared's upper lip. "My coffee definitely tastes better, though," he said, and winked.

I tossed a towel at him. "Gross."

We both laughed as he wiped the soap foam from his upper lip. I liked him: diligent, a fast learner, and a sense of humor.

My stomach growled, and I realized I hadn't even eaten breakfast. "Let's walk over to the bed and breakfast and get some lunch."

"Lunch at a bed and breakfast?"

I grabbed my sweater off the coat rack and waved for him to follow me. "There's a bistro over that way too."

He protested. "I don't really have any money. I haven't been working regularly."

"It's one of the perks." I didn't even turn around to see if he was following.

I'd hoped Hettie would be too busy at Le Bon Goût Bistrowhen we arrived for lunch, but it was too much to ask. As soon as we walked in the door, she pulled her cell phone from her bra and made a call.

Hettie now wore a fitted long sleeve black shirt and a black and white plaid mini skirt. I called it a mini because her knees were showing, not because it barely covered her butt cheeks. Her business attire could be called more conservative than her workout attire.

I had to agree with Jared, Hettie looked sexy for seventy years old, but tasteful, for the most part. Her hair had been pulled back in a simple bun at the nape of her neck. If one didn't know better, they'd think she was a respectable senior citizen.

She finished her phone call just as we were being seated, so she pulled up a chair and sat with us. Waving a hand at the hostess, she said, "Daphne, bring us a bottle of the 2007 Pinot Noir and three glasses." She looked at Jared. "You *are* old enough to drink?"

Jared reached for his wallet.

I stopped him by grabbing his arm. "No need."

Hettie looked at me. "What?"

"He's old enough, Hettie." If I wasn't pleasant with her, she'd never leave the table. Me being pleasant bored her, so I had to watch my tone. "How was your morning?"

She waved me off. "Same old, same old." She turned to Jared. "I'd like to know about your morning. How is my daughter-in-law to work for?"

Jared looked at me before answering.

I shrugged.

"It's been a fun and lesson-filled morning." He cleared his throat and drank from the glass of iced water that had just been placed on the table. "Miss Marcy's a good teacher."

I glared at him. "Just Marcy. You make me feel like a schoolmarm when you say Miss Marcy."

"Well, you have been teaching me all morning," he joked.

Hettie wiggled her brows. "Oh, I'll just bet she is a good teacher. You know she's married to my son, right?"

Jared smiled. "Actually, we haven't talked about anything personal, but I just assumed."

"I *was* married to her son. We're divorced. Not that it's anyone's concern."

Hettie reached out and put her veined hand over mine. "But they now live together in sin."

I looked Hettie in the eyes. "Is it sin if you're not having sex?"

Jared grabbed his napkin from his lap and coughed into it. Poor guy.

"Where's the bathroom?" he asked.

Hettie gave him directions as she unfolded a gold linen napkin and put it on her lap.

Great, she'd settled in.

"If you run him off, I'll make you work as my assistant," I threatened. "Or even better, I'll make Celine go to a local school, so she can continue to help me."

Hettie cocked her head. "Celine stays right where she is. She'll learn the viticulture business the right way. I won't have a man take over this empire when I die."

Hettie had set aside a large sum of money to pay for my daughter's college education. She'd made sure Celine got into Texas A&M's viticulture program with a sizeable grant to the department. Not to mention, she'd been taking on graduate students and interns for more than a decade. Queen Savoie and Texas A&M had a nice relationship.

I knew the threat would get under her skin. As it was, Celine came home almost every weekend. She wasn't acclimating as well as I'd hoped to college life. It didn't help that all her friends had stayed close to home or gone to different colleges. She'd gladly go to a local junior college for a few years and then transfer.

Thank goodness Jared hadn't fled out the back door. He came back, sat down, and picked up the menu.

The server came and opened the bottle of wine, pouring a sample for tasting into Hettie's glass. Hettie swirled and sniffed before downing the sample in one gulp. Making a show of the swirling and sniffing, the swig had been the final bow. She didn't need to taste this bottle of wine; she knew exactly how delicious it would taste.

I waited for her to bloviate on the subtle flavors and aroma, but she just nodded her head for the server to pour for everyone.

When she finished pouring, I ordered the Savoie Salad, a recipe I developed. Mixed baby greens with candied pecans, dried cranberries, toasted pumpkin seeds, crumbled feta cheese and pomegranate dressing, topped with a baked, sliced boneless chicken breast. Jared ordered the roasted portabella omelet, and Hettie waved the server away.

Just as I was expecting Hettie to start up another awkward conversation, something even worse happened. Pierre walked in the door.

I looked up and heat rose up through my face. My ears felt as if they'd been set on fire. Now it made sense, Hettie called Pierre when she saw us arrive. I leaned over and whispered, "Troublemaker."

Hettie wiped her mouth with her napkin, even though she had no reason to. She stood and walked over to give her son a hug.

Admittedly, even though I'd been married to Pierre for almost two decades, the sight of him still took my breath away almost every time he walked into a room. At six foot-two inches, he had an athletic build, tanned skin, and his blue eyes smiled even when he was pissed off. Don't ask me how I know. Pierre also had a grin that could melt even Hettie's heart. When he wasn't wearing a toque, his salt and pepper hair looked eternally ruffled, and made his sideburns look grayer.

The smile in his eyes dimmed a bit when Jared turned to see what was going on.

Hettie, being the graceful dame she pretended to be, introduced Pierre. "Jared, this is Marcy's husband, Pierre."

In stereo, Pierre and I looked at Hettie and said, "Ex-husband."

Quick to catch on, Jared said, "But you two still live together in sin."

I stifled a laugh and said, "Sit, Pierre, join us."

He pulled out his mother's chair first, and helped her get reseated, then leaned against the chair closest to me. "A new assistant?" He had yet to address Jared directly.

It wasn't like Pierre to be jealous. But then again, I hadn't even considered dating since we signed the papers, so he hadn't had the chance to be jealous. If he'd been dating, he kept that to himself. If Hettie was my mother, I'd keep it a secret, too. As for me, when I did finally start dating, I'd never bring a man onto this property.

The server arrived at the table. Lunch was served, and my stomach growled at the thought of food. Even though I worked with food all day some days, I still enjoyed eating. A little too much.

I answered Pierre's question. "Celine can only work weekends. I thought I could get by, but the blog is doing very well, and I need the help if I'm going to keep up this pace."

Pierre looked directly at Jared for the first time. "You're a blogger?"

Jared finished the last of his glass of water. "No, sir, I'm a professionally trained chef."

I saw a glint in Hettie's eye that seemed to bounce from her to Pierre. Oh, no, they were *not* going to poach my assistant.

Jared no sooner sat his glass down then the server returned to the table to refill it and smile at him. Oh, boy, this kid was going to be trouble. I needed to keep him away from the female staff.

He smiled politely back, not even aware of her interest, and said, "Thank you."

"What brings you here? I thought you needed my car today." I didn't want to start talking about food, recipes, and how much fun it was to run a kitchen. I couldn't let them know about Jared's extensive experience.

"Mom needed help with something and asked me to come right away." He looked at Hettie. "What was the emergency? You were vague on the phone."

The closed lip grin told me she'd fibbed to her son. "Oh," she waved him off, "I guess it wasn't that urgent. And then I saw Marcy and this handsome young man, and I completely forgot I called you."

Liar, liar, pants on fire. I felt like sticking my tongue out at her.

"I'm sure it will come to you as soon as I leave," Pierre said with heavy sarcasm. He wasn't blind to his mother's ways. "I've got a busy day, and I still haven't purchased the produce for tonight's menu."

"Be a dear and come to the kitchen with me," Hettie cooed.

"Mom…" Pierre knew she was up to something, and so did I. "I told you, I'm crazy busy, and Marcy will need her car back."

Hettie shrugged. "I'm sure her new assistant would be happy to give her a ride. That's what assistants do, right?"

Not taking the bait, I said, "He's not that kind of assistant, but as soon as I can afford that kind, I'll have him run your errands too, Pierre."

Pierre winked at me. "I'll be home late tonight. I'm closing the kitchen."

I smiled and said, "I might stop by for a nightcap."

Jared sat quietly, looking back and forth at us like a tennis match.

Hettie stomped off like a child who didn't get her way, and Pierre waved as he walked out.

"He tells you when he's coming home?" Jared said after they left.

"It's a courtesy since we live together. And until our daughter left for college, we raised a kid together."

Jared's lips disappeared in a frown and his brows furrowed.

"It's a strange arrangement, but it works for us." I took a long sip of wine.

"What was all of that about with Mrs. Savoie and your hus…ex-husband?"

I nearly choked on my wine. I coughed to clear my throat and said, "Hettie was snitching on me for having lunch with you."

"Why?" He still wore a confused frown on his face.

"She wanted Pierre to see I had a new *male* assistant who is handsome."

Jared looked down at the napkin on his lap.

"Sorry if that embarrassed you, but you must know how good looking you are."

When he looked up, his cheeks were painted with a dusting of pink. "I don't know about that. But I didn't mean to cause any rift with you and Mrs. Savoie."

I laughed. "Please, just call her Hettie. And not Miss Hettie, either, though we appreciate your manners. If you say Mrs. Savoie, she'll just look around the room as if you might be addressing someone else. Hettie and I have a queer relationship. I love her, and I'm pretty sure she loves me too, but she makes sure I know who the matriarch of the family is. Almost daily."

We had settled in to eat when Hettie came back to the table. "Don't be late for your meeting with Annabel. You know how she gets."

Didn't everyone know how Annabel gets?

CHAPTER 3

B ack at my studio, we finished with the coffee styling session, and I had Jared doing dishes while I pulled up the recipe for a tomato basil pesto I'd been working on. I thought it would go well with fettuccine.

"Have you ever plated a meal for photography?" I asked.

Jared dried his hands with paper towels. "Only with my iPhone. I always took pictures of the meals I made in school. Restaurants are another matter. Many have rules against photos in the kitchen."

"Not in Pierre's kitchen. They're always using Snapchat and other social media to share what goes on in the kitchen. It's sort of how I got the idea to do my food blog." I pulled the sun-dried tomatoes from the refrigerator. I should have taken them out before we left for lunch, so they'd be room temperature.

"We're working on a pasta this afternoon?" he asked.

"Yes, can you grab the fresh fettuccine from that fridge over there?" I pointed to the industrial sized refrigerator across the studio. "And I'll need some fresh basil from the window garden."

I didn't have to point out the window garden, as it was obvious. I grew my own herbs in a tiered window box. The amount of sunshine in the window worked perfectly for most of the herbs I used. I preferred growing them inside because the vineyard's Bengal cat, Lucy, loved whatever I happened to plant. She loved digging them up and pooping in the dirt. Lucy, already eight years old, had been a gift to my mother-in-law, but she was allergic, so Lucy came to live with us. In hindsight, I think Hettie wanted us to have the cat all along. Lucy didn't care that Hettie had allergies though; she helped herself to Hettie's house regularly. I stopped counting the number of times we'd gotten a call to come and get her.

Oliver and Lucy had a love-hate relationship. Lucy loved him went she wanted to play cat and mouse and be the mouse, because she always won. Poor Oliver was too big to fit into her hiding spaces, but he was patient, and he'd try to wait her out, only to fall asleep waiting.

We tried to keep Lucy in the house during the busiest times of the year, like now, when everyone was preparing for the grape harvest. Sometimes I think she hated it; other times I was sure she would never go outside again. And I couldn't wait until she was outside because I hated that darned litter box, even though we had a state-of-the-art litter box and litter. Someone still had to clean the darned thing, and guess who got that job now that Celine was in college?

"Is this for a magazine or a restaurant?" Jared asked as he placed the pasta and a small bunch of fresh picked basil on my cutting board.

"I'll need a little more basil, and I'll also need at least five perfect leaves for the photo," I said. "This is for my blog. I usually try to make three or four recipes a day and photograph them, but today, I have too much on my plate." I laughed at my unintended pun. "Of course, not every day is a recipe day. I have marketing, social media, and education days too. Oh, and ad days. Writing ad copy is the bane of my existence, but I'm getting better at it."

"So we'll be busy tomorrow then?" He brought back just the right amount of basil.

"We'll see how today goes. My meeting later may make me want to stay in bed tomorrow." I dreaded meeting with Annabel, but it was a necessary evil if we wanted the two most powerful women in the county to be happy.

"Ah, okay. Would you like me to chop the basil?"

I nodded, then added, "Except the half-dozen perfect leaves."

"I didn't cut those yet, so they'd be fresh for the hero shot."

Already using the industry jargon. I liked this guy.

As I went to gather the rest of the ingredients for my recipe, I hoped he'd be long term.

In my head, I wondered what story I would tell with this post. If you read recipe blogs, you know it's standard for the blogger to write a thousand-word article about their life and the circumstances surrounding the making of the recipe. Not to mention, the substitutions, and measurement, and anything else to make the recipe page longer, and make it harder to find the darned recipe. But the length made Google happy, and also gave more room for plenty of ads on the page.

Would I explain that the pasta had been made with my handsome new assistant? Or maybe talk about it being the first recipe for the blog that didn't have Celine's input? I missed my little girl. All my readers knew of Celine, since she'd been mentioned in posts here and there, and she'd even written a few recipes herself. I think she'd had her dad's help, but that was fine by me.

"When I interviewed you, you said you had photography experience," I said.

He continued to chop basil, then grabbed the cloves of garlic. "Minced?"

I nodded.

He pulled out three cloves of garlic and smashed them with the side of the knife blade. As he peeled the skin, he said, "I took classes in high school, but I never took it seriously. I'm good with placement and lighting, though."

"I'll do most of the lighting myself, but it's good to have a trained eye helping me." I unwrapped the fettuccine and put it next to the pot as I waited for the water to boil.

"I wouldn't call myself a trained eye, but I think I know what looks good when it comes to food. Besides, you can fix the color in post, can't you?"

I handed him the onion. "A fine dice, please." I placed the pasta in boiling water. "Like I said, I prefer to get it right in production, so I don't have to spend so much time in post. It's so much easier to get it right the first time."

I picked out a couple of Roma tomatoes to blanch after I pulled the pasta from the water and explained the recipe to Jared, handing him the handwritten card I'd made.

"You write all of your recipes by hand?" He seemed amazed.

"Why wouldn't I?" We continued prep while we chatted.

"I don't know. I guess it's easier to type into a tablet, and then you won't lose the card."

I nodded to myself. "Good idea, but I don't keep a tablet in the kitchen. I might start, though. I'd still write up the card, since I some-times photograph it with the meal. I think hand-written gives it a homey feel."

Jared had the ingredients in the food processor before I finished peeling and seeding the tomatoes. He leaned against the counter and grabbed the last tomato.

"Once the recipe is ready, we should have enough here to make four plates," I said, "That's because mistakes will get made and we'll have to start from scratch."

"And what if it's perfect the first time?" he asked.

"Then we thank our lucky stars, and we have leftovers to take home for dinner."

He grinned.

"Let's both make a plate." I explained the look I wanted.

I plated the fettuccine onto a matte black plate and twirled it into a swirl design. Then I spooned my tomato basil pesto over it and arranged the plate on a wooden mini table with a white linen napkin and a glass of "wine."

The wine was yet another stylist concoction: colored water with clear soap bubbles for a realistic look.

We had two delicious looking plates of pasta. But pasta dries out fast when sitting on a plate under lights, so I took a small brush and painted olive oil on the noodles to give them a fresh look. Once the noodles looked fresh, I spooned more tomato basil pesto over the top. Yes, it looked delicious.

I glanced over at Jared's plate, and it looked similar to mine, except he'd drizzled a bit of sauce over the side, and he'd already grated the Parmesan cheese over the top. It looked beyond delicious.

"How would you accessorize your plate?" I asked.

Without a word, he walked over to my accessories shelf and pulled out a tarnished, antique fork and spoon, along with a gingham linen napkin, and a small butcher block. He sat the butcher block on the marble table where my lighting system was set up, then put his hero plate on the butcher block. Next to the plate, he placed a small chunk of Parmesan cheese, then added a few sprinkles of grated cheese next to it. He lifted the pasta and placed the spoon under the pasta just enough that you could see it was a large spoon, then stabbed the fork into the top of the delicious looking meal at an angle. He placed perfect pieces of basil on the marble.

I clapped and grabbed my camera. "Bravo. That is clever. Anything else you want to add?"

We spent the next few hours adding and removing props from the photos and changing the lighting. In the end, we had to photograph my plate too, because we'd made a mess of Jared's that couldn't be fixed. It amazed me how much time we spent working on this photograph.

Jared had a good eye, and he seemed to enjoy the process.

By the end of the session, we'd decided Jared could take home what wasn't used for the photo, and I downloaded the photos from my camera while he cleaned up.

"Just bring back the containers. I'm forever losing them," I said.

I looked at my watch to see I had just enough time to get to Annabel's house. I wouldn't even have time to clean up and get the pesto sauce off my white shirt.

I locked the studio behind me and walked out to the car with Jared. "I'll text you later tonight to let you know what time I'll need you tomorrow."

He waved an okay as he got in his car.

Pierre had brought my Lexus back, so I hopped in and headed straight to Annabel's.

Straight might not be the right word, since driving the county roads of the East Texas was more like miles of twists and turns.

As I pulled out of the driveway, I got a text from Hettie:*Stop by Bobby Joe's office and pick up the check he owes me.*

CHAPTER 4

I thought about asking what the check was for, but I just texted back, *K*.

Bobby Joe Ryder was Annabel's husband. She ran the winery, and Bobby Joe invested the money. Actually, he invested other people's money. I'm not sure Annabel would let him invest theirs, no matter how good he was. Hettie and Annabel were two peas in a pod. Hettie's husband had died long ago, right after I married Pierre. Annabel's poor husband was dying a long, slow death. *That was mean. I didn't mean it like that. Aw heck, I guess I did.*

I pulled into the parking lot of Ryder Investments, but I didn't see Bobby Joe's Tesla. I did see a dark blue Buick 300, though. Hopefully Bobby Joe had left Hettie's check with his assistant, and I wouldn't have to come back again. I hated running errands, especially Hettie's errands. Errands were part of Celine's job when she lived at home. I missed that a lot.

I opened the door to see Bobby Joe's assistant sitting at his desk with the door half closed.

The assistant didn't look up from whatever she was doing in the desk drawers, so I said, "Is anyone here?" even though I saw the woman plain as day.

She jumped out of Bobby Joe's chair and scurried to the door. She opened it, then kicked a gym bag out from behind the door to open it wider.

"Darn it, I'd been keeping an eye on that door all day. The one time I'm absorbed in cleaning up Mr. Ryder's desk, someone moseys in. How can I help you?"

I knew Bobby Joe's assistant was several years younger than me, maybe around forty. She wore her hair in a slick French twist and dressed in a Chanel suit. Maybe it was a knock-off. No way would Annabel allow Bobby Joe to pay her enough for a genuine Chanel suit. Then again, there were some really great high-end resale stores in the Dallas area. So cynical. Maybe she got a nice bonus and wanted to dress the part for her job. But usually, the part for the job in East Texas looked a lot more casual. Like cowboy boots, blue jeans, and a nice blouse, casual.

I was sort of jealous of her slick suit. I hadn't had a reason to get dressed up since I worked as a hostess at Savoie. I hated that job, but I loved getting dressed up. It was fun to see the elites in the community stopping in for my husband's mouthwatering recipes. And it was great fodder to meet tourists. Without tourists, the wine industry in East Texas wouldn't be what it was.

I thought for a moment, trying to remember the assistant's name, but I couldn't pull it from the dusty files in my brain. I stepped up to her massive desk, which, though it was stacked high with what looked to be work and files for investors, also looked neat and tidy. I tried not to be obvious as I looked for a business card holder that might have her name.

"Marcy Savoie, right?" she said as she straightened her skirt.

"Yes," I said, hoping not to look too stupid when I didn't say her name.

"Patty Sue Osborne. But you probably don't remember me. I worked for your mother-in-law about a million years ago." Her mannerisms were so polite, I felt guilty for not remembering her name. At least she looked familiar to me. That was something, wasn't it?

"It couldn't have been that long ago, since you're not that old."

"You're too kind." She stood behind the chair at her desk. "What can I do for you?"

"I'm here to pick up a check for Hettie Savoie. She said Bobby Joe had it ready for her."

Patty Sue looked around at the stacks on her desk. "I'm so sorry, Mr. Ryder hasn't had me cut any checks for Ms. Savoie. And to be honest, I don't even know what he'd be paying her for." Her face scrunched as she thought about it.

"Could it have been Annabel who asked for the money? I'm sure it's for the Wine Train event." Not sure why she'd be perplexed about the money, since Bobby Joe had always handled the finances for the event. Then again, I was just assuming it was for the benefit.

I saw a look pass over Patty Sue's face. It was there and gone, and I didn't know if it was the mention of Annabel, or the yearly gala. I had to admit, I even got a sour taste in my mouth when the Wine Train benefit was mentioned.

"I'm sorry, I'd give Mr. Ryder a call, but he's out of town until tomorrow. And he's off the clock, so to speak." She didn't look all that sorry.

"I'll call him myself. Thanks anyway." Like hell was I calling. I'd text Hettie and she could figure out what to do.

"Oh, please, don't call. I'll take care of it tomorrow. He's taking some personal time, and really shouldn't be bothered." It was more of a pleading than a suggestion.

"Okay. You're sure he'll be back tomorrow?" I could put Hettie off and check back in the morning.

"Yes, he left yesterday. And you know he doesn't like to leave Annabel for too long. He worries about her." She sounded like an old friend of the family, not a personal assistant. It was so sweet.

"I'd want to be away from Annabel as long as I could," I said under my breath.

"Excuse me?" She leaned forward.

"Nothing, I was just thinking. I must go see Annabel now, so I'll just ask her about it." I turned to leave.

"She'll probably call me and ask why I don't have it." She still sounded pleasant, but with a hint of *that's just great* to it.

I understood exactly how she felt. It's how I felt about spending a few hours with Annabel to get the poster for benefit started. Don't get me wrong, I was happy to have the client and this event paid well, but I definitely earned it.

I left Bobby Joe's office and headed straight to the Ryder vineyards.

The Ryders grew their grapes on a different property than their other businesses. Their winery had been moved to a building on Main Street in Pear five years earlier. It had been a smart business decision, since they got walk-in traffic other wineries didn't get. Annabel had her home on the hill, just like Hettie did, but Hettie kept everything on the same property. The Ryders wanted more privacy.

Usually, I had to stop at the main gate and announce myself, but the gate was open, so I drove up the long asphalt driveway, past row after row of grapevines. The landscape finally opened up to an English style garden with a trimmed boxwood maze and circles of flower gardens.

Annabel maintained a few of the gardens herself. Her roses were her pride and joy, along with her grapes.

The garage stood to the left of the house, and I could see one of the bay doors was opened, Annabel's car inside. At least she was home. I looked at my watch. I wasn't late, so she wouldn't spend the first twenty minutes berating me and lecturing on punctuality. I'd only been late once, because of a car accident on the road about three miles from her property. It couldn't be helped. But I didn't hear the end of it. She'd probably mention it again.

I'd been coming to this antebellum plantation home on the hill since I was in my twenties. Pierre and I married while we were still in college, so these people were like family. You can't pick family, they pick you, and you get their friends too. I parked in the circular driveway in front of the house and left my keys in the car.

I walked up the cobblestone path to the front door and rang the bell. I heard it echo along the chambers of the six-thousand square foot home. Funny that I heard it. This house was well-built, and you could yell, "I'm coming" as you approached the door, and the person waiting on the other side wouldn't hear it.

I looked at the door and saw it stood slightly ajar. I frowned. Maybe Annabel really did need regular watching over. But seriously, she was only in her early seventies, and I'd never seen signs of dementia. I pushed the door open.

"Annabel?" I called out as I entered.

She might be taking a nap. I didn't want to scare the crap out of her and cause a heart attack. Not that Annabel's stone-cold heart worked that way. Oh, I was so mean. She really wasn't that bad, unless you asked her kids, all of whom got the heck out of Dodge as soon as they graduated from high school. I don't think I'd ever seen them around even during the holidays. But then again, holidays meant tourist season and busy tasting rooms, and families like the Ryders and Savoies had a lot going on at that time of year.

I called out again, but nothing. I walked into the kitchen and saw a crystal pitcher shattered on the floor. That was nothing compared to what was by the dining room window.

Chapter 5

I wanted a do over. I wanted to have called earlier in the day to reschedule the appointment. That's exactly how it should've happened. I should've been too busy with the blog and rescheduled. If I didn't get an answer, I'd have left a message. Then Bobby Joe would've been home, and I'd wouldn't have walked in on what I saw.

It looked as if there'd been a struggle. The crystal pitcher may have had iced tea in it, but now the tea, or whatever it was, pooled over the floor. In many places, it had already dried, leading me to believe Annabel had been attacked many hours before I'd arrived. It wasn't hot enough to have any fans on, so the liquid would have dried naturally. A vase of fresh flowers had fallen over on the far side of the breakfast table, Gerber daisies strewn everywhere. One had even landed on Annabel's leg.

And Annabel, sprawled out face up with her eyes wide open, stared at me from the floor. I couldn't look at her, but I couldn't look away, either. And I sure as hell wasn't going to go over and close the damn things. No dead body touching. Nope, not gonna happen.

I reached for my phone to call 911, but it slipped from my hand as I pulled it from my pocket and slid across the floor, lodging under Annabel's black pedal pushers. Really? What were the chances? I took a step forward, then stopped and reassessed the situation. No way was I going to retrieve it. From all the television shows Pierre and I watched, I knew better than to step into what could be a crime scene. But then, maybe she just had a heart attack, and reaching in to grab my phone would be okay. And then an image of Annabel grabbing my arm as I reached down flashed in my head. I was definitely not getting my phone back.

I looked around the room for a landline. Yes! An antique telephone hung on the wall. I remembered that it used to be a fully functioning phone. But again, all my television watching told me not to touch the thing. I reached across the island in the middle of the kitchen and grabbed a paper towel. Carefully lifting the receiver, I listened for a dial tone. Darn it if that thing wasn't just wall art now; no freaking dial tone.

This wasn't how I'd planned to end my afternoon. I'd planned to talk with Annabel about how unique she wanted the poster to be this year. She always wanted something spectacular, but nearly the same as the year before, so people would take notice and beg for tickets. It worked. The event usually sold out weeks in advance. And then I'd go home and enjoy a glass of wine with my previously meal prepped turmeric turkey and carrot mashed potatoes that were calling my name. My stomach would have growled if it wasn't doing summersaults.

I looked around the first floor of the house for a telephone. I felt as if I'd run a mile by the time I looked in each room. As I stopped to look for a phone, I also looked to see if anything was out of place. Then again, I'd never been given a tour of the house, so I wouldn't know unless something was blatantly in the middle of the floor or something. I found a phone in the office at the far end of the house on the first floor. I still had the paper towel in my hand and used it to pick up the receiver and dial 911.

As usual, things didn't go as planned. I wanted to call Hettie or Pierre. No way was I going near that body, and I shouldn't touch the phone again, in case there were fingerprints to be lifted. And I had to stay until the cops arrived, didn't I. I couldn't just call and leave. How would that look?

Then I remembered I had Bluetooth in my car. I stepped carefully out of the house and went back to my car, hoping my phone sitting under Annabel's leg was still within range.

I started my car, pressed the voice button on my steering wheel and said, "Call Pierre."

Yes, I called Pierre. He was my rock and my right hand. I knew I shouldn't depend on him, but I did. I loved him to the end of the earth, even if I couldn't be his wife.

"Hey, I'm kinda busy." I could tell he had me on the speakerphone. "We have a packed house tonight."

Dang it. Really bad timing. "I need you to take me off speaker. I promise I'll only take a second."

He took his phone off speaker. "What's up?" He didn't sound harried or in a hurry. He had time for me now that he'd heard the terror in my voice. And he seemed to have more time for me now that we weren't married.

Now, after ten years of barely speaking to each other when we ran Savoie's together, after he'd had an affair with one of his servers. Now, that we were just friends. Sort of.

I whispered for some reason. "I'm sitting in my car at Annabel Ryder's house. Pierre, she's dead."

"What? Did she have a heart attack?" He sounded only slightly alarmed. Even though Annabel was almost as fit as Hettie, she was high strung, so no one would have been surprised.

I mentally went over the scene in my head again, the flowers, the broken pitcher with liquid everywhere. Could she have had a heart attack? Could she have slipped and fell? Then my mind zeroed in on the divot on the side of her head, and the blood on the floor. That hadn't been caused by smacking her head on the floor. She'd been walloped hard on the side of her head.

"No. I think she was murdered." I whispered even quieter.

"What? Speak up. I swear you said she was murdered," he laughed.

I thought it highly inappropriate that he'd laughed, but Pierre marched to his own drummer.

This time, I didn't need to whisper. I was locked in my car. So even if the killer was still in the house, I had my keys in the ignition, and I was safe. I said in a normal tone, "I think Annabel was murdered."

I heard the phone drop. He must have been working and holding the phone with his ear and shoulder. He picked it back up. "Where are you right now?"

"I'm in my car in front of the Ryder house."

"Who else is there?"

"Just me and Annabel, as far as I know." I started to cry. "I dropped my phone and it's lodged under Annabel's leg."

I'm not sure why this was what made me cry.

"Holy cheese on crackers. I'll be right there. Did you call the police?" I could hear him drop something metal into something metal. I assumed it was a knife in the sink.

"I did. I'm waiting in my locked car until they get here."

"I'm on my way." I could hear him talking to his assistant chef as he put his phone in his pocket, forgetting to disconnect.

The Ryders lived way off the beaten path, and I knew it would be at least half an hour before the police arrived. Like I said, the roads are a winding mess, and you can't drive that fast.

I couldn't go back into the house, and I couldn't just sit there, so I called my best friend, Saylor Griffin.

"Saylor Griffin, how can I help you?" She sold real estate, so she always answered her phone as if it might be a client, even though the screen probably had my name showing. I doubt she bothered to look.

Reduced to sobbing, I cried into the phone. "Where are you?"

"Did Pierre cheat on you again? I'll kill that SOB," she snapped.

"He can't cheat on me anymore, silly," I laughed in between sobs.

"Oh, that's right. I keep forgetting. Are you okay?"

I told her all about what I saw, and how I called Pierre, and how he was coming to the Ryder house, but it was a terribly busy night for Savoie's.

"I'll call you right back," Saylor said.

I hiccupped a few times and stared at Annabel's roses while I waited. True to her word, Saylor called right back.

"Pierre is headed back to the restaurant. I told him I was on my way. Besides, I'm closer since you caught me at home. He tried to argue, but you know how much he likes to hang out with me, and I told him I'd be consoling you."

"Are you really coming?" I'd stopped crying and now whined a bit.

"I'm not if you don't get over this pity party you're having for yourself. It's not like *you're* dead." I could hear her moving.

"If I was dead, I wouldn't be able to have a pity party." I thought I heard hear sirens. "You don't need to come. I just needed to talk to someone."

"I'm already in the car."

"I love you," I said with more strength in my voice.

"I know." I heard the car stereo blaring Lindsay Sterling before she turned it down. "Stay on the phone with me until I get there. Hold on, I'm putting you on speaker."

Saylor talked to me about her latest real estate client to take my mind off the grisly scene inside the house. She told me how they'd given her a huge dollar amount as their buying limit, then when she started showing them houses, they'd only qualified for half the amount. Not that she cared; she just wondered why they'd wasted her time. She'd shown them half a dozen houses way out of their price range. By the time she finished describing the couple, she'd already pulled into the driveway.

Unlike me, Saylor always looked put together. She even looked elegant in yoga pants. Being almost six feet tall with legs up to her neck, she looked good in torn jeans and a plain white T-shirt. I could look that good too, I supposed, if I had any reason to. Ha, too funny. I had long red hair that refused to be tamed, and skin so pale I was almost translucent. I didn't even have the gorgeous blue eyes to offset the red hair. Just plain, dull brown eyes. When *I* wore yoga pants, I just looked too lazy to get dressed.

Saylor kept her cocoa brown hair cut short, just a bit longer than a pixie, and it always looked perfect. She was that girl everyone loved to hate, and yet she was the nicest person you'd ever want to know. If she liked you, that is. And also, if it's just the two of us, we were the cattiest women you've ever seen.

She stepped out of her BMW Z4 wearing a simple black shift dress with bare legs and black sandals. No accessories.

I unlocked my car door and got out as she walked up. She hugged me and said, "You're lucky I didn't have any showings. I'd have been halfway across the county."

I hugged her back and inhaled the clean scent of French milled soap. "Thanks for coming. And thanks for making Pierre stay at the restaurant."

She stepped back. "I promised him we'd go straight to Savoie's as soon as the police were finished with you."

"I'm exhausted just thinking about having to talk to the police. I don't really know anything. I just walked in, and she was there."

Saylor grabbed me by the arm. "Come on, I want to see."

I jerked away. "No, I don't want to see her again."

"Fine," she sighed. "I'll be right back."

I couldn't believe she just left me there. But I was *not* going back into that house. The police would have to drag me in, and I didn't think they'd do that.

I paced back and forth in the space between Saylor's car and mine, waiting to hear the sirens. I stopped and listened carefully. Nothing.

Saylor came back out, not looking a shade paler than she had when she walked in. "Girl, there's a cell phone lodged under her body. I wonder if it's hers or the killer's. She was bashed in the head; did you see that?"

I nodded and fessed up. "That's my cell phone."

Saylor stopped dead in her tracks. "What? How did that happen?"

"I was a wreck, and when I pulled it from my pocket to call 911, it slipped before I could dial. I couldn't believe it landed under Annabel's leg."

She turned on her pretty pedicured foot and headed back into the house.

"Where are you going?" I called after her.

She stopped at the open door. "I'm getting that phone. If it's not part of the murder scene, you need it. And if we wait for the cops, it will go into evidence and you'll never get it back."

Before I could protest, she disappeared back into the house. And before she came back out, a law enforcement vehicle came barreling up the driveway. No lights, no sirens. Weird. Then again, what was the hurry? No one was going anywhere.

Saylor came through the front door just as Deputy Bradley Carter stepped out of his car.

Saylor waltzed across the driveway and wrapped her arms around the deputy. She held my cell phone in her hand, and winked at me as she hugged Bradley. "Hey, good to see you." She let him go and turned around to look at the house. "Just wish it was under better circumstances."

Bradley didn't hug Saylor back. They'd had a thing a few years ago, and I think they still had a thing...sometimes...when one of them (Saylor) had too much to drink.

"What were you doing in the house?" he asked.

As if she'd just come from visiting her grandmother, she said, "I had to get a look, before you closed off the scene." She leaned in close. "You can take me in and print me later, if you like."

Damn, that girl was a flirt.

"I found Annabel, Bradley." Knowing the investigating deputy for most of my married life had its advantages, or so I'd hoped.

"What did you find?"

I described the scene again.

Saylor added, "I looked a little closer than Marcy did. There was a good struggle. Whoever did Annabel in knocked the crap out of her. Literally. I could smell it."

"Stay put. I'll be right back." He walked into the house, then came right back out. "Yeah, it's a mess in there. My backup should be here soon. Until then, I need to ask you a few questions."

I nodded, not knowing what else I could tell him.

"When was the last time you saw Mrs. Ryder?" he asked me.

"Oh, please, she'd stand up, come out here and slap you if she heard you call her Mrs. Ryder. It's Annabel." Saylor had to have her say.

"I haven't seen her in at least a week. If I remember correctly, she was having lunch with my mother-in-law at her house," I said.

"Whose house?"

"Hettie's. How else would I see her? I certainly don't drive all the way out here on a regular basis." I didn't mean for it to come out so snippy, but it did.

Deputy Carter took notes. "I don't know. Maybe you'd been here. Maybe you were here earlier today and killed Annabel. Now you're back."

I laughed to keep from vomiting. "No way. You don't think I killed Annabel. That's absurd."

He looked me in the eyes. "Is it? And then you called the cops to throw off suspicion?"

Saylor said, "You're joking, right?"

Bradley looked at her and winked. "Yeah, I'm just messing with you." Then he looked serious again and said, "No! I'm not joking. I don't know what kind of relationship you had with Mrs. Ryder."

Saylor punched Bradley hard on the arm. She had guns, so he flinched, even though he tried to act like it didn't hurt.

The deputy turned to look back at the driveway, where a convoy of law enforcement vehicles trekked coming up the road, following one another closely. I counted two sheriff's deputy cars, a DPS (highway patrol) vehicle, and two City of Pear cop cars. Six cops, including Deputy Carter? And that's only if there was only one cop per car.

I wondered if this many cops showed up for an average person's death. Annabel's contributions to the community were legendary, so this had to be big news. If it turned out to be murder, no way was this killer getting away.

Deputy Carter introduced me to his boss, Sheriff John Waters. He had been in office for eight years if I remembered correctly. He'd been a deputy for almost twenty years before running for county sheriff. I'd spoken to him at fundraisers many times. When you have one of the most successful wineries in the valley, you're a philanthropist, and Hettie Savoie was just that. Which meant I was dragged into many of her functions. Sometimes I was even Hettie's date. She never brought a man to these galas for fear of gossip.

"Marcy Savoie, what are you doing here?" Sheriff Waters asked.

"Sadly, I found Annabel." I couldn't even meet his eyes.

"That'll ruin a day, won't it?" He smiled his genuine smile, showing slightly crooked teeth.

Sheriff Waters was a big man, and not in an overeating kind of way. I'd bet he had been an offensive lineman in college. He had to tip the scales at two-fifty, and had biceps that stretched the fabric of his black polo shirt.

"Pretty much sums it up."

He looked at Carter. "Grab the crime scene tape and mark off the house." He called over to the city cops. "Ruiz, drive back down to the gate and make sure no one else drives up here. I also want you to note the license plates of anyone driving by the house."

"That could be a lot of cars," Ruiz groused. "What if I don't get them all?"

Annoyed, Waters said, "Get out your damn cell phone and take pictures. Make sure you get the license plates."

Saylor asked, "Why is he taking photos of traffic?"

"You never know when the killer may want to drive by to see if anyone has found the body yet." He looked at me. "Or the killer may have called in the body."

I held my hands up. "No, not this again. I didn't kill Annabel. I actually liked her...a little."

"She had a lot of enemies?" Waters asked.

"Besides, she may have just died," I said.

Saylor said, "Oh, no she didn't. She was murdered for sure."

"And you know this how?" Waters asked.

"Aren't you the sheriff?" Saylor asked. "Have you not met Annabel Ryder?"

"I've met her on several occasions. She's been nicer to me than her husband ever was." He looked around. "Speaking of husbands, where is Mr. Ryder?"

I raised my hand, like a kid in class. "I know," I squeaked.

He raised his brows at me. "Please tell me he's not in the house, too."

"Not even close. He's away for some personal time off. I happened to stop by his office earlier today, and his assistant told me he left town yesterday."

Carter shrugged. "That's convenient now, isn't it?"

Would Bobby Joe have any reason to kill Annabel? I'm sure she wasn't the easiest woman to live with, but he'd been with her a very long time. First marriage for both. According to Hettie, all the money came from Annabel's side of the family, and Bobby Joe had signed a prenup. So maybe he would benefit from her death, but if she'd been that bad, he'd have killed her years ago.

Come to think of it, I'd never seen Annabel and Bobby Joe cross with each other. I'd seen them in their own home, Hettie's house, out to dinner, and at social events, and they always looked happy.

Saylor stood up for Bobby Joe. "Hey, every man deserves a few days away from his wife."

"Is that how it works?" Carter asked.

Saylor ignored him.

"Stay here until I get a look at the body and catalogue the scene. Then we'll head down to the sheriff's office, and I'll get your statement." Waters didn't even look back to make sure I complied as he walked into the house.

"Are you going to be okay?" Saylor asked.

I shrugged. "As long as I don't have to go back in that house."

"Should you call Bobby Joe's office and have them get in touch with him?" Saylor asked.

"Not my circus, not my monkeys. I'm not getting any more involved than I already have." It felt selfish to say it, but I couldn't be involved.

A commotion came from the bottom of the hill. I heard a horn honk, then yelling that sounded distinctly like Hettie. I told myself it was my imagination. Then my phone rang.

"Oh, no." Saylor looked at my phone, which was still in her hand. "It's Hettie." She tossed the phone at me like it was contaminated.

I really wanted to miss the catch, and let it land hard on the cobblestone driveway. But with my luck, it wouldn't break completely, and I'd just have a shattered screen that would cut my fingers. I reached out and caught the phone just as it stopped ringing. Whew. But it was short lived. It started ringing again immediately.

I answered. "Hello, Hettie."

"Tell that stupid sheriff I'm at the end of the driveway, and I need to get up there. That is my best friend." Hettie spat into the phone.

"I'm sorry, Hettie, but this is a crime scene, and they aren't letting anyone else on the property." I felt the tension in every word, knowing a tirade was coming next.

Surprisingly, Hettie's response was calm. "Please put Sheriff Waters on the phone."

"He's not here. He's in the house, and I'm not going back into that house. Not for you. Not for anybody." I rarely spoke with authority to my family matriarch, knowing it would bite me in the butt in the long run. But there was no way I was going to call the sheriff out so she could berate him.

Turned out, I didn't have to. Apparently, Ruiz had radioed Waters. He came out of the house. "Is that your mother-in-law on the phone?" he asked me.

I nodded.

"Tell her to get her little body back in that car and go home. I don't have time for her crap today."

I held the phone out, so Hettie could hear him. I wasn't going to repeat what he'd said.

"Tell him I'll talk to him later tonight. This isn't over." Hettie disconnected.

For just a second, I wondered just how well these two knew each other. But I let it pass. I couldn't see Hettie with a man in uniform. And I couldn't see anyone in authority in a relationship with Hettie. She was way too bossy.

My phone rang again. When I answered, Hettie said, "Don't tell John that. Just don't tell him anything. I'm leaving."

John? She called him by his first name? A bit friendly, wasn't it? My suspicion was right. Hettie and John? He had to be at least ten, no, fifteen years younger than her. Go Hettie. Poor John. I snickered. And it wasn't that she used his first name. It was the inflection.

"Hettie said she'll talk to you about this later tonight. She didn't sound happy." I told him anyway. I needed to see the look on his face.

He gave nothing away and pointed at my car. "Go home. We're going to be here a while. I want to see you at the sheriff's office in two hours. If it's gonna be longer, I'll call you." He glared at Saylor. "You, too."

"What? I wasn't causing a scene. I didn't even say anything," Saylor protested.

"But you were here when I got here, so I'll want to question you, too." He pointed at the BMW, then at my car. "Go. Get out of my hair."

"What hair?" I heard Saylor say under her breath.

I smiled and got in my car, glad to be leaving. I yelled to Saylor, "Meet at Savoie? Pierre is probably pacing the kitchen."

"And Hettie will want to talk to you." Saylor opened her car door. "I got your back, girlie."

CHAPTER 6

Pierre hadn't exaggerated the reservations. When Saylor and I walked in the front door, the hostess looked overwhelmed. A petite girl in her twenties and cute as a button, she kept running her fingers over the top of her slicked back blonde ponytail and biting her lip.

Savoie's sleek interior with dark wood, polished concrete floors, and white tablecloths always got my heart rate up. So many years of working in the kitchen and hosting, I could probably do this job in my sleep, even after all these years.

"She's a wreck. Is she new?" Saylor asked.

I shrugged. I had no idea, but I didn't want my family's restaurant to look incompetent. I stepped up to the hostess desk. "What's your name?"

"Excuse me?" She looked like she wanted to hit me.

"I'm Marcy Savoie, as in Pierre and Hettie Savoie, the Savoie family. I did this job for years, and I know what you're going through. Let me help." I grabbed the pen from her hand.

She blew out an exasperated breath and stepped back half a step.

It shouldn't have been difficult, since the guests with reservations got seated first. The others would be fit in when we had room. We, as if this was still my restaurant, too. In a way, I guess it was. I got my alimony from the profits.

I couldn't seat the guests, since I looked like I should have been in the kitchen, and not as a cook, but as a dishwasher. I looked over the reservations and seating board.

"I'm Emily. I think someone gave me their name as a reservation, but they didn't really have one. Now I'm all messed up, and I have four parties waiting for a table, when they should've been seated at least fifteen minutes ago." Her little girl voice grated on my nerves, but I was here for Hettie and Pierre, not her. I'd grin and muddle through.

Looking up, I saw impatient eyes staring back at me. Before I could get another look at the reservations and the seating board, a guest came up.

Dressed in a white, starched, button down shirt and navy slacks, it looked like his collar was sharp enough to cut into his neck and he had it buttoned to the top. We were a tourist destination, so we couldn't exactly ask for a jacket and tie, but it would have kept the riff raff out. He didn't look like riff raff, but he looked like a jerk with his slicked back hair and expensive oversized watch.

"We've been waiting almost half an hour," the short gentleman growled. "How much longer?"

I reached out for his guest pager. He handed it to me. After checking the number, I wanted to call him a liar and tell him he'd just been given the block ten minutes ago. Jerk.

"Your name?" I asked with as much sap in my voice as I could muster. Goodness, I didn't miss this job.

"Olivetti," he snapped.

"Olivetti? I don't see your name here," I said as I covered his name with my thumb. "Did you give her a different name when you made your reservation?" I knew he didn't have a reservation, because reservations were written in red, and walk-ins were in blue.

"I gave Olivetti," the tension in his voice making it pitch an octave higher.

"Oh, oh, I see, you didn't *have* a reservation." I pointed to his name on the board. "If you did, your name would be in red. And as you can see, we don't have a red pen here." We did, but it was under the desk. He didn't need to know that.

"Whatever. How much longer?"

"Tell you what, Mr. Olivetti. I'll move you to the front of the list, in front of the people who called in advance and made reservations. Will that make you happy?" I fully expected him to say that would be just fine.

"No, that's not right. I just wanted to know if it'll be another half an hour or more." Less tension in the little man's voice now.

"Please, have a seat in the lounge, and we'll make sure we get you seated as soon as possible. Emily, will you find Mr. Olivetti and his party a table in the bar? Three people?"

He nodded.

I whispered in Emily's ear. "Tell the bartender that Marcy said to make his drink strong. That way he won't realize he's not getting seated."

Emily grinned and escorted the Olivetti party into the lounge.

I checked the arrangement on the board and did a quick sweep of the entire dining room. By the time Emily got back, I explained what she had available, and who could take on more than four tables at a time. I knew I could count on some servers to handle more tables than just their four-table section and not get in the weeds, while others could only handle their four-table section. When the servers had to serve soup, salad (made at the table), the main course, and dessert, along with whatever drinks the table wanted, four tables could be overwhelming.

Within minutes, the hostess area was organized, and Emily had all the guests with reservations seated. At least I'd stopped thinking about Annabel's murder for a few minutes. When I looked up, I saw Saylor standing in the corner of the lounge, sipping her signature lemon drop martini.

"You're a pro," she said as she came forward, handing me a martini glass she'd picked up from the table next to her.

I took a long sip. "I'll have nightmares tonight."

"About Annabel?"

"About being a hostess again."

We both laughed.

"Let's do this." I grabbed her by the arm and dragged her toward the kitchen.

She pulled back. "I can't go in there. I'm wearing sandals."

"You're not going into the kitchen. We're going to the office. That's where Hettie will be." I pulled harder and Saylor relented.

"I don't want to do this." She drained the rest of her martini.

"Do I have to beg?" I didn't want to face Hettie and Pierre alone.

"Tell you what, I'll be in the bar, getting a second round of martinis. You can come with me, or you can go into the kitchen, which you know will be a hot mess. Look at this place. What do you think is happening in that kitchen right now?"

She was right. The stress levels would be off the meter, and the swearing would make a hooker blush. Why would I subject myself to that? I'd already subjected myself to helping the hostess. And we'd even gotten the Olivetti party seated in less than ten minutes, so the bartender only had to overpour one round of drinks.

"Martinis it is. But remember, we still have to go to the sheriff's office in a few hours." Ugh, I had to relive the murder scene all over again. I needed the martini I held in my hand and at least one more.

The lighting in the lounge was a bit higher than the lighting in the dining room, and I saw Hettie sitting in a booth on the other side of the bar. I could count on one hand the number of times I'd seen Hettie in the bar, much less with a drink.

I tapped Saylor on the shoulder. When she turned to look at me, I pointed.

She frowned. "Should we go sit with her?"

I led the way.

I scooted in next to Hettie on one side, while Saylor slid in on the other side.

Hettie's eye makeup looked smudged, and her lipstick had been rubbed off completely.

I leaned in close. "I'm so sorry, Hettie."

Hettie took a sip of her drink. "I can't believe this is happening."

Hettie had never looked old to me before, but she looked old now. Even when she was dripping sweat from a long summer run, she still looked put together. And there I was, watching her fall apart.

"It's so close to harvest. Who's going to make sure the harvest goes smoothly?"

I leaned in close. "She has a foreman. He's been doing this for decades. And her vineyard manager is one of the best in the business. Her vineyard and winery will be fine."

Hettie looked up at me with just her bloodshot eyes. "I'm talking about the harvest in general. We always helped each other through it. Annabel, Ruthie, and me."

I didn't know what to say to that, so I didn't say anything.

"What are you drinking, Hettie?" Saylor asked.

Hettie moved her pilsner glass around on the table, moving the water ring around in a hapless design. "I don't know, some microbrew. I couldn't bring myself to drink wine tonight." She said it so quietly I could barely hear her.

"Let me get you a real drink." Saylor waved down a cocktail waitress. "Mrs. Savoie would like a lemon drop martini, ASAP."

It should have sounded snippy and rude, but somehow, with her huge smile and twinkling brown eyes, Saylor made it sound sweet. The cocktail waitress smiled back at her and rushed to the bar. Maybe it was the mention of Hettie's name and not Saylor's demeanor.

I mouthed to Saylor, "Beer then liquor, you'll be sicker."

Saylor shrugged.

Hettie leaned over and whispered in my ear. "What happened to my dear Annabel?"

Hettie and Annabel had forever been best friends. I felt bad for her and her loss.

I whispered in her ear. "I don't know for sure, but I think she'd been hit over the head. I went to meet with her for the benefit, and when she didn't answer the door, I realized it was opened. I walked in, calling her name, then I saw a broken crystal pitcher on the floor, and what looked like iced tea everywhere. Then I looked into the dining room and saw Annabel on the floor. I'm so sorry, Hettie."

Hettie said, "Annabel didn't drink iced tea. It was probably coke."

Not drinking sweet tea was a sin in the south. The fact Annabel drank coke instead of tea could have gotten her killed.

"Okay, I'll tell the police." Not that it mattered one bit, other than the sweet tea sin.

Hettie sat up straight, as if she'd had a revelation. "Hit over the head? Are you sure? She wasn't poisoned? I'd heard she was poisoned."

What? Had word gotten around town already? "Where did you hear that?"

"Pierre's sous chef told me. Pierre's been too busy to talk to me." She reached out and grabbed the martini off the waitress's tray, and nearly overturned the entire tray of drinks.

I watched in what seemed like slow motion as the experienced server rebalanced the tray, only spilling a few drops from a couple of glasses. I quietly applauded her. Then I silently chastised Hettie, who knew better than to grab a drink off a server's tray. All the credit to the cocktail server for continuing to smile. I reached in my pocket and grabbed a twenty-dollar bill and placed it on the tray without upsetting the balance.

She said, "There's a running tab."

I looked at Hettie, then to the girl and pointed at the martini. "This is a tip for that drink."

The girl's brows raised, and she walked away quickly, just in case I might change my mind.

"I was there, I saw her, and I can tell you, Pierre's sous chef has no idea what he's talking about. I'm pretty sure I didn't even tell Pierre how she died." I wracked my brain to remember my conversation with him. I didn't recall telling him what had happened to Annabel. I wasn't even sure what happened until Saylor said something about her head.

"Mmmmm, this is delicious." It was the first time I heard the slurring in her words. "I'll need another one."

Hettie never got drunk. First, she ran every morning, and no way could she run with a hangover. Second, she'd never let loose enough to lose control. Getting drunk meant giving up a bit of self-control.

I wanted to take the drink away from her, because I'd have to deal with her in the morning. Or not. Pierre would be handling her. She was *his* mother, after all. I was locking myself in my studio and never coming out. At least not until they found Annabel's killer.

I wished I'd thought of going through the house before calling the police. But then again, what if the killer had still been in the house? I might have been the next victim. Had she been robbed? Had Bobby Joe killed her, then left town for an alibi? Had Bobby Joe really left town the previous day? Maybe he killed Annabel and skipped town. I wondered if his personal time had been planned for a while, or if it was last minute. But with the floor still wet, the murder had to have happened earlier in the day. The police could ping Bobby Joe's cell phone to see if he was out of town.

"Hettie, was everything okay with Annabel and Bobby Joe?" I hadn't thought it out before I asked.

"They were married; of course things weren't okay. Being married was a problem in itself." Hettie drank half of her martini in a long sip. "My Annabel is gone." I swear I saw a tear run down her cheek right before she dropped her head and slammed her forehead onto the table.

Ouch. Crap. That was going to leave a bruise.

"Hettie, are you okay?" Saylor asked.

She lifted her head as if nothing happened. No more tears, just swollen eyes. "I'm not okay. My best friend died today. And the worst part is that we had a huge fight this morning. We had some nasty words for each other, and now I can't say I'm sorry."

Saylor looked at me. I shook my head. I knew my mother-in-law had a temper, and she was strong as an ox for a woman in her seventies. I knew I'd lose if we arm wrestled. Could she have lost it, and hit Annabel over the head in a fit of rage? I didn't want to think about it.

"What did you fight about?" Saylor asked.

Hettie shook her head. "It was nothing. The fight was so stupid."

"But Hettie, she's dead now. If you had a fight, was it a big enough fight for you to lose your temper?" I knew she wasn't going to answer Saylor, but I hoped she'd answer me.

Hettie twirled the martini glass on the table. "I don't have a temper. Annabel has the temper. She was the one who lost it on me, and I ended up leaving." Then she looked up at me, glaring. "How dare you insinuate that I might have murdered my best friend."

If Hettie didn't have a temper, I'm not sure what you'd call what Annabel had. Hettie's temper had subsided over the years that I'd known her, but it wasn't gone completely. And she held a grudge like no other. If she was mad at me, she'd bring up something I said or did before Pierre and I were even married. And she had the memory of an elephant, or selective memory when it suited her.

I touched Hettie on the arm. "I'm not insinuating anything. But you have to be honest with the police and tell them that you and Annabel got in a fight. If you don't want to share the details with me, that's fine, but be prepared to share it in minute detail with the cops. And you'd better hope that the timeline doesn't fit with when you were at the house."

Hettie shrugged. "They can just look at the security tapes to see what time I was there. And they'll hear Annabel slamming the door behind me."

That was it. Someone with money and possessions like the Savoies and the Ryders usually had security cameras. I wondered if Sheriff Waters or the deputy had noticed the cameras, and what they might have found on the video.

Not one to let something go, Saylor asked, "So what did you fight about?"

Before Hettie could answer, Pierre rushed toward the table.

"Are you okay?" he asked me.

"I'm fine, I guess. We were just having a drink before we head over to the sheriff's office for questioning."

Pierre put his hands on the table, leaning in toward me. "Questioning? What would they be questioning you about?"

"They were securing the area, and doing the crime scene investigation when I was there, so Sheriff Waters asked if I could meet him at the sheriff's office, so they can question me further after they are finished at the crime scene."

Pierre looked at Saylor. "What are you doing here?"

"Nice to see you too, Pierre." Saylor put on an innocent grin.

"That doesn't answer my question. Why are you here?" Pierre didn't let up. This was his mood at the end of a harried evening from working in the kitchen. This was the Pierre I had put up with for nearly twenty years. It had been worse when we worked together too.

I looked at my watch. It wasn't even close to the end of the evening. His poor kitchen staff.

"Saylor is here for me. You were too far away and too busy to come stay with me while I waited for the police. But you know that, because she called you. And now Saylor is going with me to the sheriff's office, because she was there at the crime scene and actually saw Annabel's body." I scooted over a bit so Pierre could sit down.

He didn't sit. Looking around, I could see the restaurant was still quite busy.

"What time are you going to the sheriff's office? And who's going to be questioning you?" he asked.

"We'll probably have another drink, then I'll call an Uber car to drive us to the sheriff's office, and back. Someone is going to need to see your mother home."

Pierre looked at Hettie. "Mom, are you okay?"

When Hettie looked up, tears were streaming down her face. "No, I'm not okay. And I won't be okay until they find Annabel's killer. Maybe not even then."

He leaned down and whispered in my ear, "How much has she had to drink?"

I grimaced at him, shrugging my shoulders, but didn't answer because I didn't know.

"Mom, how much have you had to drink?"

Again, Hettie twirled her martini glass. She waved down the waitress. "You're not my father. I don't answer to you."

Pierre's eyes opened wide. He knew his mother well, and knew she was a two glasses of wine drinker. Everyone who knew Hettie knew that she drank one glass of wine, two glasses of water, then another glass of wine. She said it was her way of stretching out the drinking and not getting drunk while still being social.

The server came over to the table, and Saylor put three fingers up and indicated to the three of us. "Another round of martinis, please."

The server nodded, scratching on her notepad and walking away.

Addressing Hettie, I said, "You were asking Sheriff Waters what was going on earlier, and he wasn't there to talk to you. Maybe you could go down to the station with us and tell him about your fight with Annabel."

"I'm not going anywhere." Hettie tilted her head back to get the last drop from her martini glass.

"I'll drive all of you to the sheriff's office, but I'm not sure why you aren't just going to the police station here in town," Pierre said.

Saylor said, "Because Annabel's home is outside the city limits, but within the county, her death falls in the jurisdiction of the sheriff's department, not the police department."

"I guess I didn't think about that. It's a good thing that Pear is the county seat," Pierre looked at his watch. "Crap, this rush is running longer than I expected. I have to get back to the kitchen."

"I'll just have an Uber driver pick us up. You need to be here to make sure everything is running smoothly. I'll bring Hettie back here when we're finished, and you can take her home." Not that home was very far, but he could at least take her up to the house, and make sure she got into bed without incident.

"Fine." I could tell Pierre didn't like the idea of us going without him. "If you're running late, just call me, and I'll come down and pick all of you up. Saylor, you should stay with Marcy tonight."

Saylor waved a hand in front of her. "Oh honey, by the time we get to the sheriff's office, finished with the questioning, and get back, I'll be as sober as a drunk who's been in AA for twelve years."

CHAPTER 7

As soon as we arrived at the sheriff's office, which held not only sheriff's personal office, but the courthouse and the jail, Sheriff Waters separated us. This made no sense to me, if we were gonna collude on what to say, we'd have done it already. We'd been drinking at the bar for over an hour, and then ridden in the Uber together. If we wanted to come up with an alibi, or a good story, we had plenty of time.

Before leaving the restaurant, Saylor and I decided bringing Hettie along was a bad idea. One more martini, and she nearly passed out at the table. She'd be useless in an interview. The bartender said he'd keep an eye on her until Pierre finished in the kitchen and promised not to serve her even if she threatened him.

They took Saylor in first, and Waters followed right behind her.

Much to my surprise, the sheriff came back out only moments later, and walked me down the hallway. "I hear Hettie's taking this pretty hard," he said.

What a strange thing for him to say. How would he even know? Then I remembered my earlier suspicion about them having a thing. I kept it to myself for the moment.

"She and Annabel were best friends." I walked beside him until he stopped at a door with his name on it.

He opened the door, letting me walk in first. "And worst enemies. They are an enigma."

Yes, they were, but I didn't agree out loud. That was a subject for him and Hettie to discuss.

I sat in the antique hardwood chair and leaned back. The chair had stiff springs, but it did rock a little, and the wheels rolled me back against the wall. I used my feet to walk the chair back toward the desk. I loved antique office chairs, even if they were torture to sit on for long periods of time. A little extra padding in the buttocks would have been nice about now.

I waited until Waters got settled behind his desk before I asked, "Off the record," I hesitated, then blurted, "Can I call you John? Or would you prefer I call you Sheriff Waters?"

He leaned back in his chair and kicked his feet up on the desk. "John is fine. Almost everyone calls me by my first name unless they're a criminal."

I laughed. "Then I'll definitely call you John."

"Is *that* what you wanted to ask me off the record?"

"No," I said. "I wanted to ask you how long you've been dating Hettie."

I think John choked on his own spit because he went into a coughing fit.

I waited. And waited. "Do you want me to hit you on the back?"

When he recovered, he said, "Excuse me. No, I'm not dating Hettie. We have been seeing a lot of each other in the last few months, but we aren't dating, per se."

"Seeing each other? Dating? Whatever. And does Pierre know about this?" I had to know if he'd kept it from me.

John crossed his arms over his chest and leaned back even further in his chair. "That's why we aren't dating. Hettie doesn't want Pierre to get upset. So there's nothing for him to know."

They were shaking the sheets; I just knew it.

"Seriously? Pierre is a grown man. And Hettie is, well, she's old, even if she doesn't know it. Who cares? Do you two really like each other?"

"We do." He grinned, cracking his tough exterior just a little. "And Hettie isn't old."

He was right, she was the youngest seventy-something I'd ever met. John probably knew how young Hettie was better than anyone.

"I'll tell Pierre." I sat up straight in the chair. "Or better yet, we can go out on a double date."

I thought this was a great idea. I almost jumped out of my chair at the cleverness of it.

"I have a murder to solve, Marcy. And the Savoie family is front and center of the investigation." His tough exterior grew right back, as if he'd never smiled.

"What do you mean, front and center?" My heart leapt in my chest, as I started to protest.

He held up his hands. "Stop right there. I'm not accusing you, just letting you know that I have to investigate thoroughly, or I wouldn't be doing my job."

Knowing Hettie and John were "friends," I had to ask. "Did you know Hettie and Annabel had an argument this morning?"

He nodded.

"Do you know what she and Annabel fought about?"

John nodded again.

"Well?" I asked.

"Not my place to discuss. Besides, I want to know more about what happened today."

I sighed. "I already told you. And I told your deputy when he arrived."

"Humor me."

I told him why I'd gone to Annabel's house, and what I'd planned to do. I explained how no one answered the door. I noticed it was open and went inside. First, I saw the liquid on the floor, then I saw Annabel. I felt like I'd told the story a thousand times already, even if it had only been a handful of times.

"And you didn't hear anything? Like maybe someone was still in the house?"

I shook my head. My heart raced. "Was someone still in the house?"

"We don't think so. If they were, they were gone by the time we went through it."

I breathed a sigh of relief. Not that it mattered now. I'd gotten out of that house unharmed. That wasn't going to change even if someone had still been in the house. I guess it was just a relief to know I wasn't being watched.

"The front door was ajar?"

"Like I said." Then I realized I hadn't paid that much attention to the door. "Was it busted open?"

"No, it doesn't look as if it was." John scribbled on his notepad.

I tried to see what he was writing, but his handwriting was small and messy. No way I could read it upside down. In fact, I doubted he'd be able to read it, either, if he hadn't written it himself. It was that bad.

Pierre's writing looked like chicken scratch, too. His employees were always asking me to decipher it. John's writing was a different kind of bad.

"No forced entry? So that means it had to have been someone Annabel knew." I wondered, with the security gate, if Annabel normally kept her doors locked. She did live in the middle of nowhere, and it wasn't as if someone could get to the house without buzzing in at the gate first. "What about the security system? If someone didn't have the code at the gate, they'd have to have called up to the house."

John shrugged. "There was a sign out front for AWC security, but we couldn't find a contact name or number anywhere. It could have been on Annabel's phone or on a computer, but she did have a Rolodex on her desk, which was torn apart, address cards all over the desk and floor. Then, we tried the online Yellow Pages and Google, and couldn't find any security company by that name. And we still haven't found Annabel's cell phone."

"Maybe it's not a local company," I said, and realized how stupid that sounded as soon as the words were out of my mouth.

"It wouldn't matter if they were from New York; they should show up on a Google search."

"That's just kind of weird. I'll have to ask Hettie if she's ever heard of them." I would expect that Hettie and Annabel had a lot of the same contacts and used a lot of the same companies. Besides, Hettie knew a lot about a lot of things. "There aren't any security signs at our place. But it's a business, so Hettie isn't trying to keep people out."

"Just another loose end," John sighed. "I'll talk to Hettie about it."

"What about a murder weapon?" I asked.

"I thought I was supposed to be the one asking the questions here?" John said.

Pushing it, I asked, "Did you find a murder weapon?"

John's lips turned up. "At this point, we aren't sure. I shouldn't be sharing any of this with you, but there is a large dent in her head, so it could've been anything from a bowling ball to a crystal vase. We're still waiting for the autopsy, but I can tell you this, whoever hit her was really strong."

I giggled. "I guarantee it wasn't a bowling ball. You wouldn't catch Annabel dead in a bowling alley. And I doubt anyone just brought a bowling ball to the house." Then I realized what I'd said was inappropriate and frowned.

"Do you know if Annabel had any enemies?"

"Annabel was a shrewd businesswoman and not always nice, so I'm sure she made her share of enemies. Nowadays, when you're in business, you never know who is going to flip out if you fire them, quit using their business services, or just say something wrong."

John nodded absently.

"Hettie has been friends with her for ages, so she'll know more."

I thought about John's strong comment. She and Annabel had a fight that morning. For a seventy-something-year-old woman, Hettie was strong. Could she have flipped out and smashed Annabel's head in?

"I'm still trying to get a hold of her husband, Bobby Joe. He's not answering his phone, and it goes directly to voicemail."

John put up his finger and picked up his cell phone that had started vibrating across his desk. He listened for a few minutes, then disconnected. "That was the crime scene unit. They just finished going over the house." He put his phone down. "As far as you know, did Bobby Joe and Annabel get along?"

"Annabel wasn't always the easiest person to get along with, no matter who you were. So, I guess they had their moments," I said.

"Don't I know it," he said, putting his arms on his desk, playing with the pen in his hand. "I've dealt with her on occasion. Even though she was nice as can be to me, she wasn't easy. I think she liked to harass me just because of Hettie."

The side of my mouth crooked up. I'd better not pursue that line, as it might incriminate me. I'd worked with her on many events over the years, too. I knew. But I also knew she wasn't so bad that someone would want to kill her. Or not. Because someone *did* kill her.

"You said earlier that Bobby Joe was out of town." It was a statement, not a question.

"As far as I know. I stopped by his office to pick up a check for Hettie, and his assistant, Patty Sue Osborne, said he was out of town. Have you talked to her?"

"We haven't. We've barely cracked into this investigation. I have her name on file but haven't called her yet. That's going to be our next step, since Mr. Ryder isn't answering his phone."

"How did you get his number?"

John pointed at his cell phone.

"You have him in your cell phone?"

"We have an emergency contingency log. We keep the phone numbers of the owners and managers of every business in the county. You never know when you'll need to call someone in the middle of the night because their property was broken into, damaged, or the barn is burning to the ground." He paused, then added, "Or their longhorns are blocking the farm to market road."

I nodded. "That's brilliant." I wondered if I was listed as an emergency contact for Pierre or Hettie. I didn't dare ask.

"That, and remember when that drunk driver went through the Ryder building about five years ago?"

I did. Sometime in the middle of the night, one of the winery managers had been tasting a little too much of his boss's product, and decided he could still drive home. He only made it three blocks before plowing head on into the Ryder building. Bobby Joe took it better than anyone expected. Annabel, on the other hand...

"Ah. You have his number from that. Makes sense. But he's not answering your calls."

"Nope." He leaned forward. "Patty Sue didn't say anything about where he'd gone, did she?"

"She didn't give me any details; just said he was out of town. Maybe he's not getting cell service where he's at." It was a plausible explanation. There were dead spots everywhere in the valley.

"I wonder when he left?"

"She said he left yesterday."

"We need to talk to Patty Sue, and we need to get inside his office. If he's not home by morning, I'm going to get a warrant to look at his calendar, phone records, and whatever else it takes to find out what's going on." He sounded irritated.

"It's not like he knew his wife was going to be killed while he was gone," I said.

"Really, how do you know that?" he countered.

That had me back on my heels. He was right, I didn't know. Maybe he'd planned it. I guess a person didn't have to be present to have a spouse, or anyone, killed.

"See what I mean?" he asked. "And maybe he wasn't really out of town after all."

"Yeah, I get it. I'm not a cop. And if you don't need me anymore, I'd like to go." I didn't even want to think about Annabel or the murder anymore. "Talk about being in the wrong place at the wrong time."

"Thanks to you, we have a head start on the murder investigation. Who knows when Mr. Ryder would have gotten home? Or who would have finally found Mrs. Ryder," John offered.

He asked me a few more repeat questions, then offered me a cup of coffee.

I asked for a bottle of water, which he grab from the mini fridge in his office, and walked me out of the room.

I sat in the waiting area, nursing my bottle of water, waiting for a glimpse of Saylor.

Finally, after a coon's age, Saylor came out of a room followed by Deputy Carter.

"Hey, sweetie."

I stood and gave her a hug. I whispered in her ear, "Did they grill you?"

She whispered back, "Not too bad. But the deputy and I got some things worked out. I think that's going to be on the recording, too."

I didn't think John had recorded our conversation. We'd been in his office, and he didn't say he was recording. Not that it mattered, in the state of Texas, only one person needed to know there was a recording for it to be legal.

Saylor waved with her fingers at Deputy Carter.

"You ready to go home?" I asked.

"I'll call a car for us," I said.

Saylor pointed and said, "No need."

I turned around to see Pierre walking through the door, looking pale and exhausted. I looked at my watch. It was nearly ten. Poor guy.

Pierre hugged me. "Are you okay?"

"It was all a formality. I'm pretty sure they don't think I killed Annabel."

Pierre stepped back from me. "Why would you even say that? There's no way they could consider you."

I didn't feel like going into it just then. "Let's go home. I have a busy day tomorrow."

A part of me wished I could forget about what had happened, and just curl up in his arms when we got home. I missed the feeling of a man's arms around me. I always said I'd start dating again when Celine left for college, but I couldn't really do it while Pierre and I still lived on his mother's property.

People who knew us probably wondered why we'd divorced in the first place. We still loved each other. We just couldn't be married. For so many reasons.

CHAPTER 8

Once we were in the car and on the road, Pierre said, "Saylor, I could just smack you across the head. What were you thinking, giving a seventy-year-old woman a lemon drop martini?"

I couldn't see Saylor sitting in the back seat, but I could hear her snicker. "She needed it. She was drinking some microbrew beer, for God's sake."

Pierre looked over his shoulder quickly and then back to the road. "The amount of alcohol in a microbrew was about what she needed, not the amount of alcohol in a martini. She was looped."

I looked at Pierre. "She only had one martini." Right? I couldn't remember for sure.

"One martini while you were there. She had a full martini sitting in front of her when I went into the bar."

I strained my neck to turn and look at Saylor. In the light of the moon, I could see the grimace on her face. "Did someone walk her home?"

"I'm sorry, Pierre. I thought she was just going to have the one drink and go back to the house."

Saylor leaned forward in the seat to talk to Pierre. "She did have a second martini in front of her when we left. And she may as well have been sucking it through a straw. It was part of the reason we decided she shouldn't go to the sheriff's department with us."

"I wasn't too worried about her getting home. I put her in the golf cart and gave her a ride back up to the house. It's tomorrow morning that I'm worried about. She's going to be furious that she got drunk, and madder than a wet hen that she has a hangover."

Saylor laughed. "It would do Hettie good to let loose occasionally. She such a control freak and so uptight. That extra martini was probably the best thing for her. Bet she's sleeping like a baby."

As Pierre pulled into the driveway of Savoie's, he said, "She's sleeping like a baby, all right. She passed out in the golf cart on the way to the house. I had to hold her in the seat with one arm while I steered with the other. Then I practically had to carry her to the house."

"Did you undress her and give her a shower, too?" I asked with a bit too much sarcasm.

"That's just gross. No one wants to see their mom naked. I laid her on the bed, fully clothed. She's going to be so pissed off the morning." He turned to Saylor. "Are you sure you're okay to drive?"

Saylor stood outside in the parking lot and walked the white line indicating the parking spaces. She put one foot in front of the other, with both of her hands out. Then she stopped and put her index finger to her nose with both hands. "Stone cold sober, my man." She said her ABCs, then said, "You want to hear them backwards?"

"Sounds like you've done this a few times," Pierre laughed.

"Once or twice. Want to give me the follow the finger with the eyes test?"

Pierre shook his head.

"We can give you a ride," I said.

Saylor reached back into the car and gave me a hug. "I'm fine. I'll text you when I get home." She walked to her car and got inside.

Pierre sat in the parking lot for a few more moments, watching as Saylor drove away. "I'm glad she was there for you today. I'm sorry I couldn't be there."

"It was for the best. You have a business to run, and she was available. You've seen me hysterical enough times in your life, and you didn't need to see that. Besides, Annabel is your godmother, and you really didn't want to see her sprawled out on the floor dead."

Pierre backed out of the parking space and headed toward our house. I'm pretty sure I saw our cat, Lucy, scuttling between the bushes, either hunting, or racing us to the house.

"I was distracted in the kitchen tonight. My assistants had to fix several of my mistakes. I kept going over in my head who would want to do this to Annabel. I know she was difficult, and sometimes kind of nasty, but she wasn't so mean that someone would want to kill her."

As Pierre maneuvered up the paved road to our bungalow, I looked out the window at the moon shining over the vineyards. I'd run over my day in my head many times.

"You know what strikes me as strange? Bobby Joe is out of town, and he's not answering his phone. Don't you think this makes him look a little guilty?"

Pierre parked in front of the garage and waited as the automatic door lifted. As he drove slowly into the garage, he said, "That is a little strange. I sure hope he has an alibi. But then again, I'm not sure Bobby Joe has the backbone to do something like this."

We got out of the car and walked toward the house. "Some people can surprise you," I said.

"That's true. My mom surprises me almost every day."

Wasn't that the truth? Hettie was the southern queen of surprises.

"Hettie said something about them fighting this morning. That they had had words, and she stormed out of the house. You don't think your mom could have whacked Annabel in head, in a fit of rage, do you?"

Pierre turned to look at me, his feet slightly spread, and his hands on his hips. "What are you trying to say? My mother is a suspect?"

I backed away from him. "No, I'm just saying she said they had a fight."

Pierre walked into the kitchen and slammed the car keys on the counter. "My mother has a temper, but she's never completely lost it. She and Annabel have been friends for years and believe me, they've had their share of fights. They always make up." Pierre turned around and opened the refrigerator, pulling out a to-go box from Savoie's.

I left the kitchen to let Oliver out of his crate. He dashed by me practically knocking me over, as I turned to head back into the kitchen. "Oliver!" I scolded him. He didn't care, he made a B-line for the doggy (and cat) door and disappeared in a blink.

"You realize I've been in your life for twenty plus years, right? And we've lived here nearly the entire time. I know the kind of fights that Hettie and Annabel have had in the past. But time goes on and people change. Maybe it was an accident. Maybe Annabel threw something at Hettie and then Hettie retaliated."

Pierre practically tossed the leftover box into the microwave and set the timer. He turned to face me. "So let me ask you this. If Annabel was dead and my mother did it, why would she admit that they had been in a fight earlier that day? Doesn't that just point the finger at her?"

"Maybe she didn't know Annabel was dead," I said. This wasn't the case, but I was just throwing it out there.

"This is all just stupid speculation. My mother is the last person who would kill somebody. The way people are these days, it could be anybody. It could be the chef Annabel fired two weeks ago, or it could be her general manager, who was suspended for having an affair with one of the servers. It could be someone who works at the winery, or it could be her husband. But I can tell you this: my mother didn't do it."

I considered pouring a glass of wine, but it was late. Instead, I filled the coffee pot with water and poured it into the machine. I measured out decaf coffee grounds into a filter and turn on the machine. "I never said Hettie did it. I just asked if it was possible. I don't have time to think about this now, I have a blog post to finish."

"You sort of *did* implicate my mother. I'm not sure you meant to, but it sounded like it to me."

"According to the sheriff, whoever hit her was strong. Hettie is short, so I wonder if she could even have that much power to hit Annabel in the head. Annabel has a good seven inches on her." I reached into the cupboard and grabbed a coffee cup. Before I closed the cabinet I asked, "Do you want some coffee?"

"Sure, I'll have a cup." The timer dinged on the microwave. "Do you want some shrimp scampi? It's leftover from yesterday. I made it and brought it home, then forgot about it. I'm surprised you didn't eat it already."

The shrimp smelled divine, so I nodded. It appeared this argument was over, but I wasn't sure, so I braced myself. I sat the coffee cups on the counter, then pulled down two plates for the shrimp. I placed them next to the microwave and Pierre doled out even portions onto the plates.

"It's going to be hard to concentrate on writing tonight." I picked up my plate and carried it to the dining room table.

Pierre followed behind me. "Then save it for tomorrow. Take a Xanax and go to bed."

We sat quietly, stirring the pasta onto spoons, and stuffing our faces. I was about halfway through my plate of shrimp when I said, "The police need to contact Bobby Joe."

Oliver came back inside, his black tail with the white tip wagging. He looked at us, then flopped down on the floor like he'd had the most exhausting day. The thing I loved about Border Collies, well mine anyway, he wasn't food driven. He'd never tasted people food, so he couldn't care less if we were at the table, eating.

"Yeah, they do."

"How?" I asked. "There's got to be a way."

"The sheriff called Hettie to see if she had Patty Sue's number. Apparently, she's not listed."

"Did she have it?" I asked.

"She wasn't in a state to respond, so I looked it up in her phone and gave it to him. I knew it was in there because I added all her contacts on her phone for her." He sounded smug.

I very nearly said something snarky, like, "Well, aren't you the best son," but that would just trigger him, and we'd have a real argument. Instead I said, "Please, your mother is one of the most tech savvy people I know. She's up on all the electronics. I doubt you put the contacts in her phone."

And that was almost as bad as being snarky.

Pierre put his fork down. "She wasn't always so savvy, you know. Twenty years ago, I put the contacts in her phone, and told her she needed to get with the times."

I'm sure he did. Pierre would never speak to his mother that way. But he had to be the best and all knowing. You see, Pierre can't be questioned, criticized, or told how to do something. It may be a pre-requisite for being a chef.

"How long has Patty Sue worked for Bobby Joe?" I asked.

He picked up his fork again and stuffed more pasta and shrimp in his mouth. He didn't respond with words, just tilted his head and shrugged one shoulder, as if to say, "I don't know."

"I hope this gets resolved fast. Celine is coming home this weekend, and she doesn't need this kind of turmoil and grief. She already wants to move back home. If she thinks there's any problems, she'll find an excuse." Celine had a gorgeous dorm room at Texas A&M, and lots of friends, but she came home every weekend. And every weekend, she looked for an excuse not to go back. I blame Hettie. Her grandmother makes her the center of her world when she comes home. And Celine gets to be in charge at the winery shop. It's a place she feels comfort-able. School pushes her out of her comfort zone.

"That's true. Hopefully, we can resolve this before she comes home. But she's got to learn to live on her own. She was self-sufficient grow-ing up, but maybe because she was at the winery so much, she wasn't as independent as we thought. College is hard, even for high school honors students, which she was not."

"Don't be so hard on her. She worked every night and weekends in the shop. Getting Bs isn't something to complain about." I got a little defensive when Pierre talked about Celine's grades.

We thought we'd done everything right with Celine. She was an good student, participated in basketball, and worked at the winery store from the time she was fourteen. By the time she was six years old, she could already work in the kitchen at home and did the dishes every night after dinner, not to mention doing her weekly chores. But she never was one to go to slumber parties. When she was younger, she tried a few times, but always ended up crying and coming home before the end of the night.

I remembered driving those horrible curving roads at eleven o'clock at night with tears in my eyes, because my little girl had called me crying.

"Remember how she'd get homesick and couldn't even attend slumber parties?" I asked.

Pierre smiled. I reached across the table and wiped some butter from his chin.

He swallowed. "She's a big girl now. She can spend the night away from home."

We'd had this conversation so many times that it made me tired. I changed the subject back to Annabel. "Do you know if she had a surveillance company?"

"What you mean surveillance?"

"Like a security company. Did she have an alarm company watching the house?"

Pierre nodded his head as he finished the food in his mouth. "She has that stupid sign at the end of the driveway. The one that says the house is protected by security. But it's not. They have that system at the gate, and they have a few cameras around the property, but it's all internal. If the house gets broken into, there aren't any police coming."

"Really?"

"Seriously, you're surprised? This is Annabel were talking about. I can remember her saying, 'What good does it do to have a surveillance company when they'll never get out here before the criminals are gone? They could back a moving truck up to the house and load all the furniture into it before the police would ever arrive.'"

It made sense that Annabel would feel this way. Even though she had more money than God, she was tight. She didn't pay for services that were a waste of money. Many times over the years, I'd heard her tell Hettie to get rid of this service or that service, "It's a waste of money," she'd say.

"So the sign is a fake, but the video is real?"

"Yep," Pierre said as he picked up our plates and took them to the dishwasher.

I stood and followed him into the kitchen, opened the fridge and grabbed the half-and-half for the coffee. I poured a generous amount in each cup, then filled them with fresh brewed coffee. "Sweetener or not?" I asked, knowing he drank his coffee a hundred different ways.

Pierre shook his head. I grabbed both cups and headed back into the dining room.

"The sheriff said Annabel's office was ransacked. Do you think they may have been looking for the video?"

Pierre took a tentative sip of coffee. "That's a possibility. But they won't find it in the office."

"What you mean they won't find it in the office?" I asked.

"About five years ago, someone deliberately erased a video, so Annabel put it somewhere no one would look. There was something on the video that she desperately wanted, and was furious that it was gone. It was something to vindicate her, I think, but I can't remember what it was."

Even more curious, I asked, "And what exactly did Annabel need to be vindicated for?"

Pierre shrugged and smiled, saying nothing.

I wanted to be mad at him for holding out on me, and for not telling me what happened at the time, but I was just too dang tired.

"Today everything is digital. She probably just has a receiver somewhere that runs off her Wifi," I said.

"Or she doesn't have anything at all." He said it like he knew something but wasn't going to share with me.

I didn't even try to drag it out of him. I was tired of talking about Annabel, but I knew this was just the beginning.

CHAPTER 9

Pierre and I had a second cup of coffee, then I decided not to work late into the night. It was a good thing, because at seven in the morning I heard a banging on the door. Jumping up out of bed, I scurried to the door, still in my pajamas. I looked down at myself just before opening the door and wondered how scary I looked. I always put my hair in a ponytail at the top of my head when I slept, and in the morning I looked as frazzled as if I'd put my finger in a light socket. My pajamas of choice the previous night had been a plain white button up shirt top and long blue pajama pants with bunnies on them. I opened the door to find Hettie standing on the porch. Thank goodness, I didn't have to care what I looked like. She'd seen me at my worst, many times.

Clad in yoga pants, a zip up hoodie, and wearing sunglasses, Hettie pushed her way into my kitchen. Oliver plodded into the room, took one look at Hettie, then did an about-face, and trotted back down the hall. Hettie didn't hate dogs, or cats, but she didn't necessarily like them either. Hettie, like her son, only liked what was one-hundred percent hers.

"Coffee and cheese biscuits, please," Hettie said. "I brought the biscuits; you just make the coffee." She lifted a box with the logo from Le Bon Gout.

Not that she had to lift the box. I smelled the divine biscuits when she walked in the door.

Hettie pulled her sunglasses from face and placed them on her head, over the hairband keeping her silver tresses from her face. She lifted the box as if it were precious and almost danced into the room.

I followed behind, stopped at the counter, and pulled out the canister of coffee beans. Measuring whole beans into the grinder, I pushed the button and listened to the sound of crushing beans while I watched Hettie's lips move. I couldn't hear a word she said, but I wasn't about to ask her to wait. Then the beans were ground and in the container, I dropped them into the reusable filter of the coffee machine and pressed the brew button.

"What's with the sunglasses?" I asked.

It took everything in me not to snicker out loud. And at the same time, I pitied her employees. I knew she had a meeting with her vineyard foreman sometime this week, and wondered if it was today. He was a bear on the best days. Now, consider putting two rank bears together in the same room, and one had a hangover. I'd stay as far from the winery as possible today.

Hettie slipped the sunglasses back a little further on her head. Getting a closer look, I realized it wasn't just the hangover that had her covering her eyes. Both eyes looked as if she'd been stung by bees, swollen nearly shut. She'd been crying last night. Probably, she cried most of the evening after finding out about Annabel, at least until she passed out. I wondered if woke up, then cried quite a bit more right before going to bed. That's what my eyes looked like when I'd cried hard and then went to bed. Lying on the bed wasn't good for the circulation.

"How's your head feel?"

Hettie whispered, "Do you have to talk so loud?" By the movement of her one eyebrow, I think she tried to wink. But it was hard to tell.

"In the future, if you plan to drink like that, make sure you take two aspirin, two vitamin B complex or B12, and a full bottle of water before you go to bed."

"Really? Because I get drunk so often?" Hettie snapped, even at a whisper.

This hangover was going to get the best of her.

"Did John call you last night?" I asked.

Hettie picked up her cell phone and looked at it. "I didn't even think about that. I was asleep. My phone blew up yesterday. I haven't answered any of the messages or read the texts."

Not sure why hearing a seventy-something year old woman saying her phone blew up actually made me think it physically blew up, and not that she's been deluged with calls and texts.

"Are you planning to?"

She put her phone on the kitchen bar. "I haven't decided. I'm seriously considering ignoring the text messages and deleting the voicemails. Unless they're from John. He might have questions relating to the investigation."

Not that it was any of my business, but that never stopped me before. I wanted to get whatever answers I could get from Hettie if she was willing to talk. I didn't think it was prudent to start my line of questioning asking about the argument Hettie and Annabel had the previous day, so I asked, "Did Bobby Joe and Annabel have a good relationship?"

Hettie picked her cell phone up and walked over to the table. She sat down, placing the phone in the pocket of her hoodie. "They were married for a long time. There were ups and downs. When you're married that many years, sometimes you hate each other, sometimes you like each other, and sometimes you want to kill each other."

I knew Hettie liked her coffee black, so I poured half-and-half in my cup first, then poured coffee into two cups and brought them over to the table. I walked back to the bar and grabbed the biscuits. Untying the box and opening the lid, I grabbed a biscuit and sat down.

"Maybe saying they wanted to kill each other isn't a good thing to mention to the cops if they come to question you."

Hettie's face cracked into a slight grin. "I'll keep that in mind."

"So, their marriage wasn't any different than anyone else's?" I asked, then took a bite of the fresh cheese biscuit.

"Yeah, but lately Annabel was acting weird. The fight? It was over the Wine Train benefit. She wanted to cancel it."

This took me by surprise. The Wine Train benefit was Annabel's pride and joy. I couldn't believe she would want to cancel this year's event.

"Why?"

Hettie sipped her coffee but didn't say anything. This was her way of telling me that it was none of my business.

"Then why did you make me go to the meeting? Why did you put me through that?"

"How the heck was I supposed to know she was going to be dead when you got there?" Hettie put her hand to her forehead.

"Want some aspirin?"

Hettie slowly shook her head.

"I'm not talking about finding Annabel dead. Why were you putting me through the aggravation of the meeting?"

Hettie moved her sunglasses back to her eyes. "I thought if you kept the appointment, she'd change her mind. I thought she'd get excited again."

"Why couldn't you just let sleeping dogs lie? This benefit is a pain in the butt. Every year, I pray that you guys will decide to end it."

If Hettie's eyes could have opened enough, she would've glared at me. Not that I'd have seen the glare since she put her sunglasses back on.

"That benefit, pain in the butt or not, brings in a lot of money. There are children's charities that depend on that money." She sighed. "I know it's a pain, but who knew it would grow in such a way? Now it's got to be an ongoing thing, or people suffer."

"Then pass it on to someone else to run. Especially now..."

I could see the hurt in her. "I can't."

"But now that Annabel is gone, you can easily pass it to someone else."

I saw a hiccup that may have been Hettie trying not to cry. "No. Wine Train is all I have left of her. It will be her eternal memorial. I can't ever let it go."

This was an argument I was going to lose, so I decided to drop the subject. I hated seeing Hettie upset, and I knew this was going to hurt her heart for a very long time. "Just don't pass it on to me," I said. "Or Pierre or Celine."

"Theres' a director's board. Don't worry, you'll never be asked to be on it."

Ouch, that stung a little, even though I was mostly relieved.

"I need to talk to John and see when they're going to release her--" she hesitated, "body. I'll help Bobby Joe with all the arrangements." She wiped her eyes with a tissue she pulled from her pocket.

"If you need anything, be sure to ask. I'll be happy to help however I can."

She nodded and dabbed her eyes again.

I wasn't sure if this was the right time, but I wanted to confirm a few things about Annabel's estate. "Last night, Pierre said the sign in front of Annabel's house, for the security company, was a fake. Is that true?"

Hettie cracked a slight smile, one that came from memories. "That Annabel, so like her. The sign is real. The company on the sign is not. They only have security at the vineyard and the winery." A little snooty, she said, "They have actual security guards working there."

So did Hettie, so I wondered why she said it with such disdain. Then I thought maybe Annabel had hired the security guards after Hettie had hired them for her businesses. Competitive much?

"But the security camera at the gate and the one at front of the house, they work, right?" Not that I didn't believe what Pierre told me the night before, but he wasn't around as much as he used to be. Maybe things had changed.

"Sure, those cameras are real."

My watch buzzed on my arm, and I could see I had a message from Jared. "Oh crap, I forgot to call Jared last night."

Hettie cocked her head. "Who's Jared?"

I stood and walked into the bedroom to grab my cell phone. I called over my shoulder, "You met him yesterday, he's my new assistant."

I heard Hettie say, "Oh, the cutie."

I came back into the dining room, texting Jared. I apologized for not contacting him the previous night and let him know we could get started as soon as he arrived.

He sent me a text back that said he could be at my studio in fifteen minutes.

"I've got to get ready for work, Hettie. Do you want more coffee?"

"I can get my own. I'm going to finish this, though, and probably be on my way. It's going to be a long day. I tried to get in touch with Bobby Joe last night, but he's not answering his phone."

My cell phone rang. I didn't recognize the number, and I usually didn't answer unknown numbers, but considering the situation, I did. On the other end of the line, was Bobby Joe's assistant, Patty Sue. As if worlds had just collided.

Her voice sounded oddly chipper when she told me she had the check ready for me.

"I thought you said you didn't want to bother Bobby Joe," I said.

"Oh, I didn't have to. I found it in my notes and made sure the check was cut. It's from an account that I sign on, so you're good to go," Patty Sue said.

I found it odd that she'd have it in her notes, but not have the check written. She'd worked for Bobby Joe a long time, if I remembered correctly. It wouldn't be like him to accept subpar performance from his assistant. Her words didn't ring true to me.

"That's great. Do you mind if I come over right now? I'm going to have a long day ahead of me, and I'd like to get this taken care of, considering the circumstances."

"Absolutely. I'm so sorry I didn't have it for you yesterday." I could almost taste the honey from her words. "I'll be here all day. Until five or six, anyway."

I took a quick shower and changed into black skinny jeans and a white T-shirt. Hettie left by the time I got out of the shower. When I thought of her losing her best friend, my heart hurt. And as much as I joked about her hangover, I wished she didn't have one. I'd have to scold Saylor for giving her those martinis. As if Pierre hadn't been harsh enough the night before. Of course, I thought he was too hard on her at the time, but seeing Hettie now made me side with him.

Jared was just closing his car door when I arrived at the studio. As I got out of my car, I saw Hettie drive past in the golf cart.

Instead of leaving Jared sitting there, because I wasn't letting him in my studio alone just yet, I decided I needed company for the drive into Pear.

"Good morning. Get in the car; we're going to drive into town quick."

Jared jogged to the passenger side of my car and waited for me to unlock the door.

"So, I didn't scare you off yesterday?" I said.

Jared's dimples showed as he smiled. "I'm not easy to scare off. I work in restaurant kitchens, and that's not for the faint of heart. In fact, I can't believe how fun fake food is."

I laughed. "Most of the food is real."

"Don't get all defensive on me know," he said.

We discussed what he'd learned from the session, and he said he might consider a food blog someday. But for now, he didn't have the self-starter abilities needed to start and stick with it. I understood that. I started and let my blog lapse at least a dozen times before I got serious. And in hindsight, I kick myself for not sticking with it from the start. I'd have two or three income producing blogs by now.

I pulled into the nearly empty parking lot at Ryder Investments and parked right by the door. "Want to go in with me? I'll just be a minute."

"Thanks, I'm good," he said and lowered the passenger seat back a bit.

Really? A nap? Already? It wasn't even nine yet.

Patty Sue stood at her desk with the check in her hand when I entered the building. "I'm so sorry. I just heard about Annabel."

She didn't look all that sorry. But she did look frazzled.

Her tone sounded different from her tone on the phone.

I took the check from her and asked, "When did you find out?"

"The police were just here. I thought you sounded strange on the phone. I guess I didn't notice because I was in such a good mood when I called you." She couldn't seem to figure out what to do with her hands, so she sat down and put them in her lap. "The police sure changed my mood in a hurry. It's all just so tragic."

"I did think it was strange that you were so chipper. But then again, I had no idea whether the police had contacted you, or Bobby Joe."

"Apparently, they couldn't reach me yesterday or last night. And no one has been able to get in touch with Bobby Joe. I guess I forgot to tell you that he doesn't take his cell phone with him when he takes these little trips. He has another cell phone that he takes, one that isn't for business. I don't think very many people have the number."

But I'll just bet you do, I thought.

The look on my face must have said a lot, without me saying anything.

"Oh, I know it sounds strange. But he doesn't want to be bothered with business when he takes his vacations. Annabel has the number, I think. If she hadn't been the victim, she would've been able to get a hold of him."

"Would the number have been on her cell phone?" I asked before remembering the police hadn't been able to find Annabel's phone.

"I don't know." The snippiness in her voice wasn't masked well. "I didn't look through Annabel's cell phone. I didn't work for Annabel."

"How did you feel about Annabel?" I asked. Her smug attitude had me thinking she didn't much like her.

"Oh, Annabel was fine. I didn't deal with her much. And from what I hear, that's a good thing. Working for Bobby Joe has always been a pleasant experience." Patty Sue rearranged the paper clips and sticky notes on her desk. "It bothers me that people think I should know everything about Annabel just because I work for her husband."

"Speaking of Bobby Joe, did you get a hold of him?"

"Yes, he's on his way home now. He was madder than a snake that married a garden hose when I called. But when I told him the news, he just went silent, then said, 'I'm on my way.'"

Patty Sue stood again and walked around to the front of her desk, staring at the parking lot. "Who's that with you? That's not your husband." Then she squinted and looked closer. "Don't that just beat all you ever stepped in? That's Jared Guidry. What are you doing with *him*?"

I looked out the window at Jared in the passenger seat, his head barely visible, then turned my attention back to Patty Sue. "What do you mean?"

She came around the desk to stand next to me. "Jared used to work for Annabel. He was a sous chef at The Poached Pear, but he was fired for stealing."

My breath caught in my throat. His resumè said nothing about working for Annabel.

Trying to bond with Patty Sue and get more information, I said, "Well, butter my butt and call me a biscuit! Are you sure it's the same guy? I didn't see The Poached Pear on his resumè."

If Jared had been paying attention, Patty Sue would have made him balk. Her arms flailed as she said, "How could you not know? He was bilking Annabel and Bobby Joe for thousands of dollars."

"And how exactly was he doing that?" I wasn't sure how a sous chef could steal that much from a restaurant.

"You'd have to ask Annabel, I mean Bobby Joe, about the details. It was really convoluted. But when Annabel fired him, it was a knock-down, drag out fight." Patty Sue punched at the air.

It was funny to see this woman, in her pale pink suit, slicked back hair, and perfect makeup, punching the air like a boxer. Girly punches. I was embarrassed for her.

"In what way?" My curiosity got the better of me and I wondered if I should let this kid be in my car.

Kid. Who was I trying to fool? He was in his twenties. Not a kid by any means.

"It was a screaming match. Jared denied everything, then the general manager got involved. It was a mess. Annabel made it clear, under no uncertain terms, that Jared would never work in an East Texas restaurant or winery ever again. She told him everybody was going to know what he did."

"What was her proof?"

"Like I said, you'll have to ask Bobby Joe. But I can tell you this, he wouldn't be working for me."

Patty Sue walked back around to her desk and sat down. The phone rang and she answered.

I had the check in my hand and didn't really need to know anything else from Patty Sue, so I waved and exited the building. I'd get it straight from the horse's mouth. When I got in the car, I didn't say anything to Jared. I didn't want to have a scene right there in the parking lot for Patty Sue to see. I drove back to the studio, and when he got out of the car, I asked "Why didn't you tell me that you'd worked for Annabel? I didn't see that work experience on your resumè."

Jared stopped dead in his tracks and turned to face me. "Of course not. I wasn't going to put that on my resumè. Annabel tried to ruin my life."

"What exactly happened?" At least I had the chance to get two sides to the story. I'd have to decide where in the middle the truth lay.

"I was fired for stealing. She said she had proof that I had stolen money from the restaurant. I've never stolen so much as a piece of bubble gum in my life, and here she was accusing me of stealing thousands of dollars."

"What was her proof?"

Jared threw his hands in the air as if giving up. "I didn't stick around much longer to find out. Once she told me that she was going to ruin my career as a chef, I'd had enough. I told her where she could stick her accusations, I got in my car and left."

"She had to have some sort of proof. She couldn't just fire you based on suspicions."

"Queen Annabel thinks she rules the kingdom. She told me there wasn't anything I could do. She knew it was me, and that's all she needed. I considered taking her to court, but I was a jobless chef and she was, well, Annabel Ryder."

I totally understood where he was coming from. Annabel could bankrupt him, and it wouldn't put a dent in her fortune. Sad state of affairs of the court system.

Jared's body sagged and he leaned against his car. "I'm telling you; I wasn't stealing. I'm sure the general manager set me up. It wasn't pretty. Annabel scolded and cursed at me, saying I'd never work in the East Texas again. She wouldn't listen to reason. I tried to explain how, as a sous chef, I didn't even have access to steal that much." He sighed and ran his hands through his hair. "Even if I *was* a the position, I wouldn't do it."

"That must've made you mad," I goaded.

"As horrible a woman as she is, I thought she was all talk. But I didn't want to take a chance, so I applied for the job here."

I thought about what he said, and unless I had proof, I had to take him at face value. But I did have one question. "Why were you late yesterday? I mean the real reason."

Jared pushed off the car, his body stiffened. "Why?"

He seemed truly perplexed. I wondered if he knew, or he was a good actor.

"Annabel is dead," I stated bluntly. "She was murdered."

The surprise on Jared's face looked genuine. Maybe he was prepared for this moment and had practiced that face.

"Oh my gosh. What happened?"

I ignored the question. "You see why I could think you had reason to want her dead?"

"I can't say I'm sorry she's dead, but it wasn't me."

"You have an alibi?"

Jared reached for the door handle on his car. "I don't need this. I don't need an alibi, either. I had nothing to do with Annabel's death."

"Before you storm off, you should know I'm not firing you. I'm not sure that I trust you, but I can't fire you until you've been arrested and charged. The police are going to come talk to you, and you'd better have an alibi."

Jared slammed the door to his car. "I told you; I was in my car. I fell asleep because I'd had a late night the night before."

That was exactly what he told me. And he repeated it almost word for word. But it didn't make sense. It didn't the first time either. "You're saying no one saw you yesterday morning?"

"No, I was alone."

"You know what, Jared? This isn't going to be a good day to work. I'll pay you for five hours because you came in, but I just don't have any work for you today."

Jared's face went slack. "So you *are* firing me?"

"No, but I don't think I'm going to get much work done today, so it'll be a waste of your time to have you here. Why don't you be here by eight o'clock tomorrow morning unless I call you and tell you otherwise?"

Jared shook his head, got in his car, and slammed the door. His wheels spit gravel as he drove away.

How on earth did I end up knee-deep in Annabel's murder?

CHAPTER 10

I didn't see Hettie's golf cart at the bed and breakfast, so I walked up the hill to her house. The golf cart was parked in its designated space next to the four-car garage. And Pierre's car was parked next to that.

Hettie must have still been feeling crappy. That she admitted it to me that morning was a miracle. It implied lack of control. That's something she rarely admitted.

Pierre opened the front door of the sprawling rainch style home and held it open. "What brings you to the top of the hill?"

Top of the hill is more like high ground in Texas. We may have lived in the Piney Woods, but we didn't have much for hills and no mountains. The Savoie home overlooked acres of grapes. Such a beautiful sight, except during the winter when the vines look like gnarly arthritic hands. Just before harvest, as they were now, they looked full of life and color.

I looked behind me at the hustle of the farmhands prepping for harvest. The vines, with green and purple grapes, that looked ready to burst. The rows of vines grew right up to within a hundred feet of Hettie's home.

"I came to talk to your mom. How's she doing?" I walked past him and into the foyer.

Every time I walked into Hettie's home, I was reminded of almost any episode of MTV's *Cribs*. You'd expect a grape theme, considering the money that built this house, but I think this was Hettie's retreat away from grapes. The entry had dark wood paneling like you'd see in an expansive home library, and a nine-foot ornate wooden table, with a massive flower arrangement that changed weekly and partially blocked the view down the center hall. I couldn't say I was a fan of the birds of paradise arrangement I saw when I walked in. Not that the arrangement wasn't nice, it just wasn't my favorite flower.

"She's in her bedroom. She says she's fine, but as long as I've been alive, she's never missed a day of work." Pierre closed the door and followed me into the entry.

"I'm going have a chat with her." I walked past him to the far corner of the house.

Hettie had built the ranch home as one expansive single story. Yes, building up was less expensive, but they weren't that worried money, even 30 or 40 years ago. She wanted a home she could live in comfortably until the day she died. And even though she ran at least five to ten miles almost daily, she hated climbing stairs.

Pierre jogged up to me and grabbed my hand. "That's probably not a good idea."

I yanked my hand away. "I'm a big girl. If she turns me away, I'll handle it."

He stood planted in place with his hands on his hips, and watched me walk into the lion's den.

I knocked lightly on the door. "Hettie, are you okay?"

I heard her strong voice through the heavy wood door. "Go away."

I opened the door and walked in. I found her sitting in front of open French doors, rocking in an antique wooden chair. "I said go away, not come in."

Mine and Pierre's bungalow would fit in Hettie's bedroom twice. The room had heated marble floors with expensive antique rugs placed strategically under her bed and under the sitting area. She'd gotten them on a visit to Hong Kong. Her bed was to the right of the door and boasted a silk diamond-tuck headboard that stopped just short of the twenty-foot ceiling. It was framed in blond wood that matched the nightstands. To the left of the French doors, which opening onto a deck as large as the room itself, was a sitting area complete with antique chairs, coffee table and a couch. The color theme of the room was beige, and tasteful in its ornateness. Faux marble columns graced the edge of the deck, where the roof ended. There she sat with the French doors wide open.

October in Texas brought cooler, if not cool weather, and even though wasps, flies, and mosquitoes still hovered, they didn't hover at Hettie's house. Having a gardener with an aversion to insects and snakes meant he kept all the pests at bay.

Next to her walk-in closet, she had a custom-made vanity and bench. Unlike most of Hettie's furniture, this wasn't antique. It had been a gift from her husband. He's apparently said she took so long getting ready it was the only time she stopped in one place long enough to have a conversation. So he had two rocking chairs made to match the style of the vanity. And he'd enjoy her company while he drank sweet tea and enjoyed her company.

I pulled a chair from her vanity and sat next to her. "Maybe you need to go for a run. Sweat all of the toxins out of your body."

She looked at me and I saw her red swollen eyes. If possible, they looked worse than when I saw her earlier. "If I ran, I'd puke. Or dry heave. I hate throwing up."

I wasn't a big fan of vomiting, either. Or running, even though I'd been known to indulge.

"I'm so sorry about Annabel. I really am. I know you've been friends forever. This is a horrible way to lose her."

"I've cried so much that my eyeballs hurt." Hettie sniffed and rubbed her eyes with the back of her hands. "I just hope we find the loser who did this."

I put my hand on the arm of Hettie's rocker. "You remember my assistant?"

Hettie looked at me, but didn't say anything.

"Did he look familiar to you at all?"

Hettie frowned. "No, why?"

"You said something about him being at the gym where you have a membership."

"Oh, that's right. I thought maybe I'd seen him at Stretch's place. So I guess he looked vaguely familiar."

I took a deep breath before saying anything, then just blurted it out. "Patty Sue saw him earlier today and said he used to work for Annabel. Apparently, she fired him. She had accused him of stealing thousands of dollars from her, and it ended in a nasty fight. Annabel swore to him that she was going to ruin his career, and that he'd never work in East Texas as a chef ever again."

"Oh, yes, I heard about that. But I never met the guy. This kid working for you, that's him?"

I nodded. "Yes, according to Patty Sue. He admitted getting fired and Annabel screaming at him, but not the stealing. He swears up and down he didn't steal from her. What do you think?"

Hettie went back to staring out the window at her vineyards. "Annabel didn't say too much about it, other than that one of her employees had been robbing her blind." She gave a sardonic laugh. "Like anybody could rob Annabel blind. She was so rich; she makes us look poor."

I didn't know about her *us* comment, but *I* was definitely poor compared to the Savoie or the Ryder families.

"He doesn't seem like the type of person who would kill her. But if she tried to ruin his career, he may be vengeful." I thought for a moment. "I've only known him a day. Anyone can be someone else for a day. Or even for months. He could be good at hiding his real personality."

"Annabel is the vengeful one. You didn't want to cross her. I just feel so bad that our last words weren't friendly. You know, like I'd never have told her that I've got to go because I've got something better to do, if I'd known it was going to be the last time I'd talk to her."

I understood exactly how she felt. The day before my dad died, I'd been talking to him on the phone, and it had been the best conversation in years. I didn't want to hang up, but Oliver had had a vet appointment, so I told him that I had to go. If I'd known, I would've skipped the vet appointment and talk to him for hours.

"I can't fire this guy based on Annabel's accusations. Do you think there's a possibility that someone else could've been stealing from Annabel?"

"There is a possibility. I remember Annabel saying something about not being so sure after she let her sous chef go. But the money stopped disappearing once he was gone."

I shrugged. "That doesn't mean anything. It just means that whoever was stealing had to stop because their scapegoat was no longer there."

Hettie turned her head slowly. "Can we talk about this some other time? I'm not in the mood for conversation."

I stood and put Hettie's chair back at her vanity. "Thanks for your time. I was just wondering if you heard anything about the theft at the Poached Pear."

"I'd heard about it, but I don't know all the gory details. Just what I told you."

"You don't, by any chance, have the key to Annabel's house, do you?"

Hettie's head quickly turned, and I could see it hurt her. She looked as if she was waiting for the nausea to subside before she said, "What do you want the key to Annabel's house for?"

I stood next to her. "I want to look around. Maybe there's something the police didn't notice that I might."

"How many times have you been in Annabel's house? And just what do you think you're going to notice that the police didn't?"

She was right, but I knew Annabel was fastidious, and anything out of place would not be the norm. Did the police know that?

"Look, I just want to get a look at her house. Maybe there's something. I already feel bad that I didn't see the ransacked office. Don't you want this murder solved?"

"I don't see how a failed chef and food blogger is going to be anything but a hinderance."

"Hettie, that's rude," I said. I cringed, waiting for the fallout. No one talked back to Hettie Savioe.

Shockingly, Hettie jabbed her finger toward her nightstand. "There's a key in there. But I think the police know what they're doing. Sheriff Waters is quite capable."

I smiled to myself. *Yes, I'll bet Sheriff Waters is quite capable.* I so wanted to say it out loud.

I went to her nightstand and pulled open the drawer. There were several keys, but Annabel's was easy to find, because it had her name on it.

"What about the key code for the gate?"

Hettie wasn't sure if the code had been changed, but she gave me the one she knew.

"I hope you feel better soon. Pierre is worried about you. He says you've never missed a day of work."

Hettie stood up and turned to me. "And I won't miss today, either. I'm just running a little late."

CHAPTER 11

I had so much to do at home and in the studio that I didn't know why I was getting myself involved in Annabel's murder. I was behind on blog posts, recipe development, and my food photography. But there I was, driving out to Annabel's house.

I felt like I'd made up for lost time at work by listening to a blogging podcast on the way to the Ryder home. I'm not sure about other places, but in Texas, just up the road could mean a few minutes drive, to an hour drive. We didn't much think about the distance between places. *"How far is it to Austin?" "Just up the road about five hours."*

Stopping at the gate to punch in the code Hettie had given me, I waited as the gate opened. I drove up the long driveway and didn't see any cars parked in front of the house. I wondered if Bobby Joe had come back yet. He'd surely park in the garage.

I parked in front of the house, in the same place I had when I was supposed to meet with Annabel, and walked to the front door. Putting the key in the door, I looked up at the video camera, and wondered if it was working.

Placing my key in the lock, I turned the handle and pushed the door open to see Bobby Joe standing right in front of me.

My heart leaped into my throat and I may have screamed. I definitely screamed. "You scared the crap out of me."

Bobby Joe, like Annabel and Hettie, was in his seventies, yet he looked about fifty. He stood a smidge over six feet tall with an athletic body. I knew he was a runner, but with his broad shoulders, he must also lift weights. I'd only ever seen him in a long sleeve business shirt, with a tie, and dress pants, so I didn't know what was under that fabric. As he stood in front of me now, he wore a polo shirt and plaid shorts, as if he'd been on a golf course.

"I should hope so. What are you doing in my house?"

"Oh gosh, Mr. Bobby Joe, I'm so sorry. I didn't know you were already home. Miss Hettie gave me the key so I could look around. I wanted to see if I could find any evidence the police might've overlooked." I could have smacked myself up beside the head. I shouldn't have told him why I wanted to look around. I should have made an excuse and come back later.

Bobby Joe took a step toward me. "So, you're in the investigation business now?"

"No, I was just thinking we knew Annabel better than the police, and maybe if I looked around, I'd see something they hadn't." I wondered if I should ask him about the video, but thought I'd wait until he was more amicable.

"I don't think it's necessary, but thank you." He walked toward the door and held it open for me.

I had no intention of leaving. "Do you mind if I ask, how were you and Annabel doing?"

Bobby Joe slammed the door shut behind me. "I do mind if you ask, but I can tell you things weren't good."

I stopped breathing to keep myself from gasping. This was a revelation.

"Not good?" I tried to sound sympathetic, not curious.

"It's not public knowledge, but Annabel and I are in the middle of a divorce. Or, *were* in the middle of a divorce." Bobby Joe looked as if a pin had popped his inflated balloon.

"Oh goodness, does Hettie know?"

Bobby Joe shook his head. "No, no one knows. That's how Annabel wanted it."

"You know this looks really bad, right?" I said.

Bobby Joe walked through the foyer and toward the bar. It was still morning, but he poured himself two fingers of scotch. He drank it down, then poured two more. "That's just it. My killing her would do me no favors. What I would've gotten from the prenuptial agreement would have been more than I'll get now she's dead."

Just to make sure he understood I wasn't going anywhere anytime soon, I sat down on the loveseat across from the bar. "How does that work?"

Bobby Joe downed his second drink, then leaned against the bar. "In the prenuptial agreement, I get a percentage of what Annabel and I earned in the lifetime of our marriage. But according to her will, I get nothing from the estate. It will be sold at auction at fair market value, and the proceeds will go to charity. She had three charities named in her will, but I can't remember which ones they were. I can tell you this: she left nothing to her family members."

Whoa. I knew Annabel was selfish, and estranged from her family, but this took the cake. "She's not even leaving anything to the kids?"

"She made that quite clear when they decided not to go into the wine business. She told them many years ago, under no uncertain terms, they wouldn't get the winery or the income from it once she was gone if they weren't working here."

"And she was true to her word."

Bobby Joe nodded.

"But you are still living together, even though you're getting a divorce?"

Bobby Joe walked behind the bar and rinsed out his glass. "It was amicable. She was ready to move on, and so was I. These last ten years have been rough."

"Have you talked to the police?" Not that it was any of my business, but that hadn't stopped me yet.

He shook his head. "Not in person. I spoke to them on the phone this morning."

"Do they know about the divorce?"

"They will soon enough. The sheriff has asked me to come down and see him at the sheriff's office." He looked at his watch. "I'd better get going. Let me show you out."

This was not what I wanted. I needed time in the house alone to look around. And I needed to know about the video. "Pierre told me you have a security system, but it's not with the company on the sign."

"Yes, we do. It's our own private system because really, what good does it do to pay someone all that money just to have them tell you you're being robbed? We live in the middle of nowhere. By the time the police arrived, burglars could've taken everything from the house and been long gone."

"Pierre said something about hiding the surveillance system?"

Bobby Joe chuckled. "Pierre knows a little bit about everything, doesn't he? He's definitely Hettie's son. The grape doesn't fall far from the vine."

I laughed. "Isn't that the truth."

He gave a light chuckle. "We had a video system in our office, but someone came in and deleted everything. There was evidence on the video that would have exonerated Annabel in a lawsuit. We did eventually win the suit, but it was many thousands of dollars later. Since then, we have kept the system hidden." Bobby Joe washed his hands and dried them on a towel that he threw into a hamper. "Come on, I'll show you."

I followed Bobby Joe up the stairs, and into a small room that looked like a den or office. He pressed a button and the bookcase opened. Behind the bookcase was a small room with a split screen monitor and two computers.

"So you didn't have a digital, Bluetooth system? The kind where you can see the video on your phone?"

Bobby Joe stopped and turned back to look at me. "No, no, not for Annabel. She didn't want her personal business on 'the cloud.'"

I understood that. I sometimes wondered who had access and could see my personal life.

"This is it."

"Have you looked at the video from yesterday?"

"No, I just got home about an hour ago. I haven't even had time to think about it. Processing Annabel's death has been harder than I thought it would be. Even though we couldn't live together and were divorcing, I still loved her."

"Do you mind if I look through them?"

Again, Bobby Joe looked at his watch. "Look, I need to go talk to the sheriff. And I'm not leaving you in this house alone. It's bad enough Hettie has a key to the house."

"Well, do you mind if I download the footage and watch it from home?"

"I don't know what you'll find, because the camera is set to delete old activity. It's deleted from the mainsystem, but it's on an external drive somewhere. I don't know how to get into the hard drive. The cameras are motion activated, so they don't run all the time, but you might be able to get something."

I reached in my purse and showed him I had a flash drive. "I can download it onto this in a matter of a minute or two, if you let me. And I can go over the video while you go talk to Sheriff Waters."

Bobby Joe wore a resigned, almost perplexed, look on his face, as if he didn't know whether to tell me yes or no. After almost a minute passed, he said "It won't delete what's on there?"

I shook my head. "No, it won't affect anything, just make a copy of it."

"Fine, make it quick. I need to get out of here."

"You can go ahead and go, Mr. Bobby Joe. I'll just download the videos and be on my way."

"Please, you're practically family. Just Bobby Joe. You've known me forever."

"Bobby Joe," I said.

Bobby Joe shook his head and left the room. "Make sure you shut the bookcase before you leave," he yelled back as he walked down the hall.

I stuck the flash drive into the video system's drive, looked up the necessary video files, then downloaded them. Not knowing which one would have the information I needed, I hoped I had enough room on the drive to download recordings from both systems. Once the first one was finished, I pushed the flash drive into the second one and asked it to do its thing. As much as I wanted to look around the house and see if there were any clues, I thought it would be best to just leave. Bobby Joe was cooperating so far, and I didn't want him to stop. As soon as the second set of videos finished downloading, I placed the flash drive back in my purse and left the room, making sure the bookcase was closed tight. I mentally patted myself on the back for having the willpower to leave the house without snooping. But as I headed back into town, I smacked myself up beside the head for chickening out and not searching the house. I'd driven halfway into town when my phone rang.

I glanced at my dashboard quickly to see who was calling but didn't recognize the phone number. Fully expecting it to be a robocall, I almost ignored it. At the last second, I decided to answer. "Hello."

I put the call on speaker, since it's illegal to have your cell phone in your hand while you were driving. A voice came through the speakers of my Lexus.

"Mrs. Savoie, you don't know me, or at least I don't think you know me, but well, I don't know." She rambled.

"Who is this?" I tried not to sound testy.

"Mrs. Savoie, my name is Breanna Toomey, and I'm a friend of Jared's."

I didn't see this going well. "What can I do for you, Breanna?"

"Jared told me Annabel Ryder is dead. And he told me he's a suspect."

"I don't know if he's a suspect or not. I just know he and Annabel didn't end their relationship on a positive note." I tried to be friendly, even though I was irritated. Maybe she had something to tell me.

"Jared told me what he told you, that he didn't have an alibi. But he does have an alibi. It's me. We were together yesterday morning. He just didn't want to tell you who he was with."

That didn't make any sense to me. If he was with a girl, why wouldn't he tell me? I didn't respond, waiting for her to fill the silence.

"He didn't want to tell you he was with me, because, well, I'm still married."

Just great. First, he allegedly steals from my mother-in-law's best friend, and then he's having an affair with a married woman. I needed to start doing more thorough background checks before I hired anybody in the future. And character references. I considered the best way to do that.

"What would it have mattered if he had told me he was with someone? I don't care if you're married or not."

"Jared and I have been trying to keep it a secret until I can get away from my husband. And because it's frowned upon at the Poached Pear. If my husband found out, Annabel wouldn't be the only person who is dead."

But Jared didn't work at the Poached Pear any longer, so why would anyone care? Well, he did allegedly steal from them. "How do you know Jared?"

"We worked together at the Poached Pear. He used to give me rides home because my husband didn't trust me to let me have the car. Guess that backfired. When we got off work early, we'd hang out together and eventually, we started sleeping together. My husband works nights, so sometimes Jared and I would be with each other until the morning."

The story sounded plausible enough. "What you're saying is Jared does have an alibi?"

"He does. I'm his alibi. And even though it puts my life in danger, I'm willing to come forward."

The more I thought about it, I felt gullible. Such a convenient story. "I don't care what you do. I'm just his employer. He may not even need an alibi, for all I know."

"I wanted to come forward as soon as possible, before things blew up."

I thanked Breanna and hung up. My mind reeled as I drove back to my studio. I could not wait to get into the studio and watch that video. I needed to see who had come and gone from Annabel's house. Was one of those people Jared?

But I had just one more stop to make.

CHAPTER 12

I pulled up to the back door of the Poached Pear and let myself in through the kitchen entrance. I'd done this many times in the past, so it wasn't something new to me. I wanted to get there before they opened for lunch.

I walked down the dark hallway and turned left where the hall gave way to the main kitchen. I eased past the dishwashing station and prep areas and knocked on the door of the manager's office.

The sterile white walls and stainless steel never quite made up for the smell of the garbage disposal when the kitchen was closed. During work hours, the aromas of cooking overpowered the odors of what didn't get eaten. The tile floors and rubber mats held onto what they knew. Even though the floors were thoroughly cleaned, hosed down and sanitized every night, the smell lingered. I'd spent enough off hours in restaurants to know the smell before it hit my nose.

Most restaurants didn't waste valuable square footage on their offices, but Annabel didn't mind. She had plenty of room to expand if needed, and the Poached Pear offices were huge and luxurious. I wished Hettie had the same idea of office space Annabel had. In Hettie's defense, neither Pierre's restaurant or the bistro had enough room for a spacious office, and adding on might take away from the integrity of the charming buildings. It's hard to match the brick of old buildings these days.

The door opened, and a tall man with a thick middle stood in the doorway. He wore faded blue jeans and a thin white undershirt. His head shined under the florescent lights. Even though he didn't look happy to see me, his hazel eyes twinkled, and his thick lips had a hint of a smile, like he knew the answer to a joke I wasn't in on.

"Hi, I don't think we've met. I'm Marcy Savoie." I stuck out my hand.

Reluctantly, he put his hand out and shook mine. It was half-hearted. Instead of giving me his name he asked, "Savoie's?"

I nodded. "Sort of. My mother-in-law and ex-husband own Savoie's."

"Aren't you in enemy territory?"

I heard a snorting noise behind him.

"Ha, right. I'm looking for Alejandro Luna." Alejandro was the Poached Pear's head chef.

He stepped back and pushed the door to shut it and I put my foot in the frame. I wasn't going to be dismissed. I'd learned a thing or two from Hettie over the years. This conversation would be over when I said it was over.

"He doesn't come in for the lunch shift." The man looked down at my foot.

"I'm sorry, who did you say you were again?" I wasn't sorry. I felt my hackles going up at his rudeness. Annabel would never have put up with this.

"I didn't. But I'm the assistant chef, they call me Billy." He relented and opened the door a bit wider. "Do you want me to leave a message for Alejandro?"

"Maybe you can answer my question." I didn't wait for him to say he couldn't. "Did you work here when Jared Guidry was the sous chef?"

His brows raised and for the first time, he looked interested. "Why are you asking?"

The other person in the office approached and opened the door wide. "Who's asking about Jared?"

I grinned. "He applied for a position with my company, I was passing through town on my way back to Savoie Winery, and thought I'd stop by for a verbal reference." I hoped I sounded truthful.

"That's a good one." Billy laughed.

"What do you mean?"

"You don't know what happened?"

"I'm guessing if I did, I wouldn't be standing here. That is, if you're talking about Jared." I played dumb.

"He was fired for stealing," the young woman said. "Annabel really let him have it."

I introduced myself again. "Hi, I'm Marcy Savoie."

The woman's face went pale. "Oh, uh, I'm Breanna."

Ah, she was something. A cute little thing with an hourglass body and nice cleavage. Her tanned skin looked well maintained, and I'd bet she had no tan lines. Even her pixie haircut had a bit of sass.

She didn't seem as protective of Jared in this environment. Dog eat dog in the restaurant business. I wondered whose ass she was covering for.

"I was the one who brought it to Annabel's attention," Billy said, sounding proud. "He'd thought he'd gotten away with the big rip off.

Annabel didn't even ask for the money back. She just told him to get out of her face and she'd better never see him again."

"How did you know it was him?" I asked.

Breanna looked at Billy, who looked back at her. Then he turned to me and said, "We aren't supposed to discuss the details because of security issues."

What a crock of crap. I wanted to say as much.

"Have you hired a new sous chef?" I asked, instead of saying what I really wanted to say.

"We have. Not hard to find good chefs when you're a world-renowned restaurant." He looked smug.

I knew that wasn't exactly the case. Dallas restaurants paid much better than East Texas. It was usually about timing. But chefs did tend to be a bit more reliable than other restaurant help.

"I'd really like to know what happened. I guess I'll just call Annabel." I took a chance Breanna wouldn't rat me out, since I hadn't given her up.

"I hardly see how that's going to happen. Annabel was...she died yesterday." He looked down, as if he felt bad for saying it out loud.

"That's what we were discussing when you knocked on the door," Breanna said. "There will be so many changes now that she's gone. We'll be needing a new general manager, and there will be changes in the kitchen. So much to take care of with her gone."

"Are you in management?" I asked Breanna.

"Actually, I oversee the wait staff." Her chest inflated just a bit.

I wasn't sure what to think of this girl. She had to be close to thirty. She deserved to be called a woman.

"Are you getting a promotion, too?" I couldn't help but wonder about her stake in Annabel's death. She looked strong enough to smack Annabel in the head.

"I don't know what will happen next," she said. "Would you like me to walk you back to your car?"

I was finished for the time being, so I nodded.

Once we were out of the kitchen, Breanna said, "Look, no one knows about me and Jared. I can't lose this job. At least not yet. Please keep our secret."

"I'm cool," I said as I opened my car door and got in.

Breanna watched me as I drove away.

I had no desire to hurt anyone, physically or monetarily. I wouldn't spill her secret unless I had to. And after what I heard in the office, I wasn't sure I believed any of it anyway.

I wished I'd learned more from Billy, but I didn't know any more now than I did before.

I pulled out of the parking lot of Poached Pear, then turned onto a side street and called Savoie's. When the manager answered, I told him who I was and that I needed Alejandro Luna's phone number. I hoped he'd have it. Luck was running on my side and he gave me the number.

"Do you want me to text it to you, so you can dial it from the text? That way you don't have to write it down," he said.

I thanked him, and pressed the phone number on the text message when it came through.

Alejandro's phone rang three times then went to voice mail. I thought that was weird. Most phones ring at least five time before switching over.

I left a message. "Hi, this is Marcy Savoie from Savoie's. I wanted to talk to you a little bit about Annabel, and what happen with the sous chef she fired. Please call me back."

After I disconnected, I realized it was a stupid message, but I wasn't going to call back and leave another one.

Frustrated, I went home to view the videos.

CHAPTER 13

When I pulled into the driveway, Jared's car was parked outside, and he was leaning against it. He walked up to my car, and before I could even get out, he opened the door and asked, "Did Breanna call you?"

"As a matter fact, not only did she call, I saw her, too. So this married woman you're having an affair with is your alibi?" I wanted to see if he was sticking to the story.

"Now do you understand why I couldn't tell you where I was?"

I still didn't get it, so I asked him, "Protecting her from her husband finding out about her cheating was more important than keeping yourself out of prison for someone's murder?"

"You don't understand, he's dangerous. For all I know, *he* killed Annabel. He would probably blame Annabel for Breanna and I getting together if he knew. But I *can* tell you this, if she had to supply me an alibi and it became public, he'd kill her. Like I said, he's dangerous. And besides, I didn't steal anything from that woman. I'm innocent on both counts."

I believed him, sort of. If only he hadn't seemed so animated. It reminded me of when people just keep talking and give you so much detail that you start to wonder if the detail is to throw you off the lie.

"Tell me the truth. Why did you apply for a job with me?" I wanted to know if it was to get closer to Hettie and Pierre, and maybe get into Savoie for a sous chef job.

"I did lie to you before. Annabel did follow through on her threat. She made sure I didn't have a reference to get another job as a chef. I even applied at Savoie's and was turned down. But while I was there, I heard a rumor you were looking for someone with cooking experience to help you in your studio. That's why I applied for the job. I can't afford to move, and I have to pay the rent. As it is, I have three roommates. How on earth was I going to be able to afford a cleaning deposit and first and last month's rent if I move? I needed something right away."

This was the first thing he said that sounded completely plausible. I just stared at him. Nothing like being told you were the last resort.

"See? I'm sincere. I want this job."

I touched him on the shoulder to reassure him. "I'm not going to fire you, but I'm not going to have you work today. I'm working on things you can't help with. I'll call you and let you know if I need you in the morning. If you don't hear from me, text me. It just means I forgot, not that I don't want you to work."

The look of relief on Jared's face was as if his girlfriend of two months had told him the pregnancy test came up negative.

There were so many inconsistencies I wanted to ask him about, like why wasn't Breanna wasn't wearing a wedding band. Not to mention, there wasn't a tan line. Weird for a woman whose husband was so jealous.

I waved him off as he got back in his car and drove away.

Jogging up to the house, I was out of breath before I got to the door. Dang, I needed to start getting more exercise. Once inside, I unlocked Oliver's kennel. Huffing and puffing, I said, "Let's go."

He didn't need to told twice, he ran past me to the back of the house to do his business. I caught my breath then walked to my studio. I didn't have to worry about Oliver follow, as I was his person. When he could he preferred to be my shadow.

I unlocked the door, then locked it behind me, even checking to make sure it was locked. I didn't want anyone walking in on me and seeing what I was looking at, especially if it was the killer. I didn't want to be the next victim.

I hurried over to my computer, pulled the chair out and sat down before taking the flash drive out of my purse. Oliver practically tiptoed up beside me and lay down with his paw on my foot. I smiled and scratched behind his ears, then hit the enter button on my keyboard and my computer came to life. As soon as it booted up, I pushed the flash drive into the slot and waited. I had to click through to several files to get to the videos. Once I was in the file, I saw a list of videos. Cool, my flash drive got it all. I was new to this flash drive thing. I'd had to learn it so I wasn't taking up so much room on my older laptop.

Since I didn't have an exact timeline, I started at the top and looked at everything. There were several ten second videos that showed nothing. And then I saw Hettie. The video showed her going into the house, apparently being invited in. That's when I realized I didn't have the sound turned on. I turned the volume up just in time to hear the door close. The next video showed Hettie back on the porch, storming out of the door. A second later, the door slammed behind her. She was already off the porch by the time the door slammed, so someone in the house had to have closed it behind her. To me, this vindicated Hettie. Annabel must have closed the door behind her after the fight.

The next recording showed a timestamp about thirty minutes later. After Hettie had left, a hooded figure approached the house and entered with the key. From the angle of the camera and the dirty lens that made it grainy, I couldn't tell the exact size of the person entering the house, or if they were male or female. I'd have to remind Bobby Joe to clean the lenses on his cameras. Then I remembered there were two sets of recordings, and I scrolled forward to find the recordings for the front gate. There were a lot of short videos from the driveway camera that didn't include someone at the gate. I did find the video of Hettie arriving and leaving. Oddly, when Hettie left, she didn't have to wait for the gate to open because it was already open. I thought that was strange. Then I remembered the gate was open when I arrived at Annabel's house. I didn't think much of it, figuring Annabel was expecting me and had opened the gate for me. The more I thought about it, Annabel would never have left the gate open. And there wasn't any video of another car coming up to the gate or the driveway. So where did the hooded person come from? I looked through the rest of the short videos until I saw my car come to the gate. I knew what happened from there.

I pulled the flash drive out of the computer and locked it in the small safe in my wall. I wanted to be sure no one else could get to it. If something happened to Bobby Joe's copies, I'd still have mine. I looked around my studio to see that all the windows were still covered. I hadn't opened the shades. Normally, I'd open them all for the beautiful light I could use for photographs. But that morning I wasn't photographing anything, so I left the shades closed. In fact, I wasn't doing anything money earning. This murder, which it had to be murder, had me so distracted.

I wondered if Hettie had made her way down to the bed-and-breakfast. Oliver wasn't allowed in the restaurants, so I left him in the studio. When he was younger, I'd have never left him loose. I'd made that mistake and spent the entire afternoon cleaning up the pillow innards and shredded fabric. He'd even killed all his favorite stuffed animals.

"You behave," I said, as if he understood me.

Walking out of my studio, I locked up behind me, and headed over.

Inside the bustling bistro, I saw Hettie sitting with Ruth Blue. If ever there were Three Musketeers, it was Hettie, Ruth, and Annabel.

"Ruth, I haven't seen you in forever." I open my arms and hugged her tight. Ruth was my favorite friend of Hettie's.

"Hey sweetie, have a seat. I just returned from Italy, and I've been telling Hettie all about it." And then her face went solemn. "And Hettie's been telling me about Annabel. It's a horrible loss."

For just a moment, I wondered if Ruth had returned today or yesterday? Did Ruth and Annabel have any sort of falling out recently? I mean, these women could go at it. Then I shook the thought from my head. No, not Ruth.

The waitress came and sat a glass of water in front of me. "Will you be ordering also?"

I shook my head and thanked her.

"Isn't that Annabel's granddaughter?" Ruth asked.

"Yes, she's been working here for about a month," Hettie said.

"That's Abby Watson?" I asked. "Why isn't she working at Annabel's place?"

"You know Annabel. No such thing as nepotism. And there's bad blood, so Annabel wouldn't hire her. Abby's mom, Emma, moved back to town, and Abby needed a job."

I remembered what Bobby Joe had said about Annabel disinheriting the kids, and the rift over no one wanting to take over the vineyard and restaurant.

"How furious was Annabel that you hired Abby?" Ruth asked.

"Not at all. She didn't care if I hired her; she just wasn't going to have the girl working at her place." Hettie's eyes welled up. "Annabel beat her drum to a different set of sheet music."

I frowned at Hettie's drum reference.

Ruth put her hand on Hettie's forearm. "Sweetie, I know this is hard on you. Let's not talk about Annabel. We'll have plenty of time to mourn her at the funeral."

"When is the funeral? I hadn't heard anything about arrangements."

Ruth still had her hand on Hettie's forearm, and she put her other hand on mine. "There haven't been any arrangements. But there will be a funeral."

"I talked to John this morning, and they're keeping Annabel's body for a while, in case they need to do more tests," Hettie replied.

"So she won't have a funeral, or be laid to rest, until they find her murderer?" I asked.

Ruth shook her head. "No, I don't think it works that way. But they probably are just being cautious for now."

"Hettie, Celine comes home this weekend. I don't want her embroiled in all of this," I said.

Hettie glared at me. "Celine's not a little girl anymore. She needs to know things like murder happen."

I shook my head vehemently. "Not yet she doesn't. I'm sure she's aware, but she doesn't need to know it happened to someone she knows. I sure hope the police have this resolved before she gets home." I glared back at Hettie. "Don't you dare call her."

Hettie waved me off with her hand. "Oh, please, I have better things to worry about than whether or not Celine finds out about this murder. I have a business to run. Harvest is right around the corner.

And I've never been happier to be busy, so I don't think about my egregious loss."

The anger had turned Hettie's face red, but tears didn't well up in her eyes when she spoke about Annabel this time. Back to my good old Hettie.

"I was just talking to Bobby Joe. Did you know Bobby Joe and Annabel were getting a divorce?"

The shock on Hettie and Ruth's face looked as if they'd seen a ghost.

Ruth was the first to speak. "That's just not possible. Bobby Joe and Annabel were the happiest couple I know. When my Robert died, I was so sad, and I know Bobby Joe must feel the same way about Annabel."

Hettie just shook her head.

"I just came from talking to Bobby Joe, so I got it from the horse's mouth. They've been working through the details of the divorce and hadn't quite finalized it. He said it was amicable. There was nothing to contest since he signed a prenup all those years ago. And he is devastated at the loss, even if they were divorcing."

Again, Hettie shook her head. "No, that's not possible. Annabel always told me everything. If she and Bobby Joe were getting a divorce, I'd have known."

"When was the last time you saw them together in public? And I'm not talking about seeing them at the same charity function, because that would be normal. When was the last time you saw them standing next to each other, hugging, and holding each other's hand?"

Ruthie clucked. "We just aren't of the age were public displays of affection are a thing."

Hettie said, "I don't know. I see couples our age holding hands all the time."

Luckily, neither Ruth or Hettie had used Botox, so I could easily see the frowns on both of their faces.

"Come to think of it..." Ruth said.

Hettie looked at Ruth. "You know, you're right."

I wasn't sure what they were talking about, PDA, or Bobby Joe and Annabel.

"Right about what?" I asked.

"They hadn't been all that affectionate. I remember Bobby Joe used to kiss Annabel on the forehead once in a while," Ruth said.

It took every ounce of energy not to smile. I loved knowing more than they did.

"On another note, but still on Annabel: when you arrived at Annabel's house yesterday morning, Hettie, did you have to use the gate key code to get in?" I asked, because there was such a short hesitation on the video, and it didn't look like she'd entered a code.

"No, Annabel opened it from the house," Hettie said. "Why? I gave you the key code. Didn't it work?"

"It worked all right. But I was wondering if the gate was still open when you left, or did you have to wait for it to reopen so you could leave?" The angle of the camera didn't show the gate. It was pointed in the direction of the road.

Hettie looked at me as if I was crazy, then I could see the wheels turning in her head as she contemplated. "Actually, the gate was already open, as if it hadn't closed after I arrived."

"And what about when you came back to the house, after you heard about Annabel's murder? Was the gate open then?" This had to lead to something.

Again, her wheels were turning. "I can't be sure, because I was more fixated on that patrol car at the end of the driveway. But I'm pretty sure the gate was open." She looked at Ruth and then back at me. "Was it open when you went to go see Annabel?"

I nodded.

"I wonder if there's a glitch in the gate?" Hettie said, incredulous. "Annabel was so careful about security. I can't remember the gate ever being left open, even when she expected a delivery. And since her home was separate from her vineyard, that wasn't often anyway."

My head was spinning with possibilities. Could whoever killed Annabel have had a key to the house? No, there was enough hesitation of the hooded person on the porch that someone answered the door. But I didn't notice a knock on the door. I wondered if Annabel saw a person had arrived and just opened the door. Could it be someone she knew? Once the person stepped inside, the video stopped. It was motion activated.

"I need to stop worrying about this. It's not my job to solve Annabel's murder. But there are just some things I can't get out of my head. And I know Annabel was very particular about that gate," I said.

Ruth swallowed a sip of water and set her cup down. "Annabel, she was a bit paranoid. Always afraid someone was after her and her money."

"True, but being paranoid never hurt anyone. It pays to be careful. That's why I keep in shape. If I'm ever attacked, at least I'll have a fighting chance to get away."

"And here I thought it was all vanity," I said.

Ruth laughed. "That too. You know Hettie too well."

Hettie took as sip of her water as the server came back to the table. "Ready to order?"

I wondered if Hettie had said anything about the murder to Annabel's granddaughter. If she had, the girl didn't seem too broken up about it.

She had a genuine smile as she took our orders and returned to the kitchen.

I thought about asking Hettie but decided to wait until after lunch.

CHAPTER 14

I needed to focus on work and not on solving Annabel's murder. That had been my mantra for the last hour. Investigations of any kind other than the ingredients in a recipe weren't my line of work. I'd been impulsive in quitting my full-time food stylist job, and I needed to make this blog profitable. So far, it was doing well for what it was. But I needed to find something to make one of my posts go viral. As of yet, I hadn't figured out how to make that happen. And I didn't have the personality to make videos for TikTok.

I learned all about search engine optimization, great layout, and branding myself, but I was still building the page views. Under one-hundred thousand page views a month just wasn't cutting it, and wouldn't let me get away from food styling clients. Until the blog could be self-sufficient and support me, I'd still need to take on clients. My goal was to only style food for myself in the future. I needed at least three more blog posts to get ahead of my week, and not having an assistant for the day wasn't going to help. The whole point of hiring an assistant was so the blog would grow faster, and I could concentrate on making it more profitable. But here I was, all by myself, working. Or not working, since I'd gotten all wrapped up in what happened to Annabel. And why? Just because I was the person to find her? We had law enforcement for a reason, so laymen didn't try to do the work of professionals.

As I looked through my refrigerator and cabinets to see what I could use to put together a recipe, I kept thinking about who could possibly have killed Annabel. I'd shake my head to clear the thoughts, but then my brain went right back to it. Bobby Joe said he would be better off if Annabel were alive. Was this true? Or did he gain from a life insurance policy he hadn't declared yet. I was sure the police would find out sooner or later. And what about Jared? Why did he have his girlfriend call me? Why didn't he just tell me himself? Did he think it would sound more legit if it was coming from her?

I needed someone to bounce my ideas off, so I sent Saylor a text: *What are you doing after work?*

Saylor: *I was going out for drinks with you.*

I laughed to myself and responded back: *Where do you want to meet?*

Saylor: *Poached Pear.*

I told her I'd meet her there. It would be great to see what the atmosphere was like in the restaurant since Annabel's death. In the meantime, I had recipes to develop.

With what I could find on the fly, I decided to make it a sandwich day. I'd make my Open-Faced Chicken & Cranberry Salad sandwich, my favorite Cucumber Avocado Sandwich, and last, because it was so messy, my PB&J with Brie Cheese on grilled flatbread. Cranberry chicken salad is a southern favorite, and even though the recipe is slightly different than mine, the bistro marks it as a bestseller. I loved open-faced sandwiches. This would be fun and quick. And I'd pair the recipes with a fun and bubbly Prosecco, or maybe one of Savioe's blackberry wines. My mouth watered. Hopefully, I'd have leftovers I could eat when I was done. Or maybe I'd make two of the Cucumber Avocado sandwiches so I could eat one while I was working.

I plugged my phone into my studio speakers and set Pandora Radio to smooth jazz, then jogged over to the door to make sure it was locked. Jazz was perfect for working, so I cranked it. For some reason, music with lyrics distracted me, and the last thing I needed was another distraction.

I had yet to open the shades in the studio, so I went around opening every single one, and even opened a window to let some fresh air in. The lighting couldn't have been better for photography. Just overcast enough the shadows wouldn't be too harsh. I moved my photography table over to the window, then went back and grabbed my camera and tripod.

I think every photographer has a different way of setting up their photos. I had my table, props, lighting set up, and my camera. The camera was on a tripod to prevent movement when taking the shot. I wasn't steady enough to take the photographs with a handheld and get the quality I needed. I also had a new articulated arm I used for overhead shots, and planned to use it when I began doing food videos. The older I got, the harder it was to see the image on the LCD screen of my DSLR camera, so I had spent some money for an external monitor. I had the monitor facing my food table, so I could stand right in front of the food and adjust, rather than fixing, going to the camera to check, then back to the table over and over. This saved a good amount of time when I didn't have an assistant available.

Once I made the recipe and plated the food, I changed the depth of field several different times for several different shots. I had to see the photo on my computer screen to decide which one I'd finally use. I'd pretty much worked like this for my entire photography and styling career. I was self-taught and I knew my early pictures were bad, but practice makes better. I'd say perfect, but I didn't think artists ever thought something was perfect.

I looked over to the articulating arm I wasn't using and yearned to start shooting videos. I hoped I could do something just different enough my videos would go viral. I'd been trying to think of "out of the box" ideas to stand out from the rest of the awesome food bloggers on the internet. But for now, I didn't have time to play around with videos.

Today, eating a sandwich was my way of recipe testing, and it was yummy. I set to work on making my tasty morsels after I had the camera and lighting set up, and the accessories picked out. Knowing I was going to be going out with Saylor, I refrained from tasting the wine. Yes, this time I actually had real wine on hand, usually provided by wineries who wanted me to mention their labels in my posts. A nice perk, except I had access to all the wine I wanted at home. Though I did love drinking wines from a variety of wineries, not just Savoie. Since I'd expected it to be a quick photo shoot without a lot of time under the lights, I poured a glass of the blackberry wine for the photo shoot.

The PB&J&B was as messy as I'd expected, but in my mind messy equaled delicious. I didn't taste test this sandwich because I'd made it before at home. I didn't consider how messy it would be, but I think I got some fabulous shots. Blackberry wine with that sandwich for sure.

By the time I finished the photo shoot and wrote the blog post, it was time to meet Saylor at the Poached Pear. I cleaned up my studio and put the dishes in the dishwasher, but I didn't have time to change clothes. I checked my shirt for any signs of mayo, jelly, or peanut butter. I was all good. I tossed my apron in the hamper and disconnected my phone from the speakers. Locking up my studio and jogging out to my car, I drove into the main hub of the little town of Pear, Texas. I turned right on Main Street, and immediately on the other side of the street stood the Poached Pear.

As I drove by, I saw Saylor walking on the sidewalk, so I roll down my window and waved. "Be there in a minute."

Saylor waved back and disappeared behind the large front door.

I didn't go to the Poached Pear often and now; this had been my second time in one day. Once inside, I was informed Saylor had already ordered for both of us. We'd been friends long enough we each knew what the other liked.

Saylor sat at a comfortable booth in the corner of the bar, holding the small wine menu.

"I ordered us the 2004 Cabernet. And I just finished ordering an appetizer, a simple tomato bruschetta."

I flopped down on the seat across from her, feeling almost exhausted. "Thank you. One less decision I have to make today. My mind is fried from thinking too much."

Saylor cocked her head and looked at me. "You? Thinking too much? You're a blogger, for goodness sake," she laughed.

"Annabel's death has me by the heart and mind for some reason."

Saylor looked perplexed. "I didn't think you even liked Annabel. Every time you had to meet with her about the benefit, you complained."

I shrugged. "I didn't dislike her. I just didn't like working with her on the benefit. Annabel is a lot like Hettie: her way or no way. She never allowed us to be innovative unless it was her idea. I always wanted to try something new and different with the posters, and she refused. I swear to you, even with a new recipe on the posters every year, they all looked the same. How could they be collectors' items if every poster looked so similar? Besides, she was Hettie's best friend and I feel for Hettie. She's having a hard time with it, even though she's putting on a brave face. At least in public."

The bartender brought our glasses of wine. Saylor took a long sip. As the bartender walked away Saylor said, "I guess you don't get the same service in the bar you get in the dining room."

"What do you mean?"

"I bought a bottle. He should've opened the bottle in front of me and let us taste it."

Saylor's snippy voice made me think she'd had a long day. "Are you sure you ordered a bottle?"

The bartender hadn't brought the bottle to our table.

Saylor grimaced. "Fine, maybe I said two glasses."

"I can't have more than a glass anyway. I have so much to do. When I get home, I still have two more blog posts to write up." Who was I kidding? I wasn't going to do any more work for the day.

Saylor took another sip of her wine. "What have you been doing all day? Don't you have an assistant now?"

I told her about what had happened with Jared and how I had let him go for the day. I explained to her I'd been snooping around at Annabel's house and hadn't gotten much of anything done. "I did make and photograph three sandwich recipes, though."

"Wow, you outdid yourself," she laughed.

I stuck my tongue out at her and changed the subject back to Annabel. "Did you know Annabel's granddaughter is working for Hettie?"

Saylor's brows raised. "And how would I know that?"

"Don't give me that, Saylor. You know pretty much everything that goes on in Pear and the surrounding county."

Saylor grinned from ear to ear. "Not everything. I haven't heard about this. How long has she been working for your mother-in-law?"

Even Saylor still called Hettie my mother-in-law. Old habits, I supposed.

I had no idea. And I didn't see how it was relevant, so I didn't answer. Instead, I told her about how I had talked to Bobby Joe, and what he told me about the divorce.

"Divorce? How did I not know about this one, either? That would be the talk of the county." Saylor unfolded her napkin and placed it in her lap.

"I guess Bobby Joe and Annabel thought the same, so they kept it very hush-hush. I don't know what part of the process they were in, but it was going through, according to Bobby Joe. What I wouldn't give to see those divorce papers."

The appetizer was served, and Saylor was quiet until the bartender walked away again.

"I can tell you this: you aren't going to see anything now. If the divorce had gone through, the papers would've been public. That would have been an interesting read." Saylor picked up a bruschetta. Absentmindedly, she added, "I wonder if I would have gotten the listing on the house?"

I shook my head and stuffed my mouth full of food to keep from admonishing her for the selfish thought.

When the discussion turned to the surveillance videos and how I'd seen Hettie arrive and leave the house, Saylor forgot about the food. She sipped her wine and stared at me.

"You didn't really think Hettie killed her in the first place, did you?" she asked.

My mouth was full now, so I shook my head. I really didn't think Hettie would do such a thing. She had a temper, but not like that.

When I told her about Jared and the phone call I got that morning, Saylor stopped drinking, too. She was mid-sip and she just stopped.

"So what do you think?" I asked.

She put her glass down. "Do you believe him?"

"Why shouldn't I?" I wasn't sure if I believed him or not, to be honest. "I don't know him at all. And I hadn't heard anything about there being a theft here at the Poached Pear. Something like that would get around even if they tried to keep it quiet. Someone gets fired and people talk."

"I hadn't heard of it, either." She acted like she didn't care, but I knew better. This conversation was making her feel like she was out of the loop, I could tell.

"It's not like we talked about personal stuff during the one day we worked together, so I wouldn't have had any idea if he even had a girlfriend. But he told me he'd fallen asleep in his car while listening to music that morning. That made me think he was homeless. And the story just didn't quite ring true."

Saylor moved the wine glass around on the table, staring into space. After a moment she said, "Check his phone."

"Check his phone for what?"

"Check his call log," she said.

"And what am I going to find from his call log?" I wasn't quite sure where she was going with this.

Saylor never ate much, but she liked to pick at her food. And she was now picking at the appetizer, pulling out the bits of tomato and popping one at a time into her mouth. "If they *are* dating, there will be lots of calls and texts back and forth. So, if this girl is legitimate, you'll see her number on his phone. Do you have the number?"

I pulled my cell phone out and looked at the call log. "Yeah, sure, she didn't block the number, but it was a number I didn't recognize when the call came in. I have it here." I showed Saylor the screen.

"Then you need to get into Jared's phone and see if there was a lot of communication between him and this girl."

Before I put my phone away, I sent Jared a text, telling him I would meet him first thing in the morning and to be there by eight.

"Now, how do you get into his phone?" Saylor chewed too long on a tiny piece of tomato.

I thought about that. I'd bet he had it password-protected. If it was, it would be virtually impossible to unlock.

I finished the rest of the appetizer and swallowed the last of the wine in my glass while Saylor told me about the different rumors going around Pear about Annabel's death.

"I've heard it was suicide; that Bobby Joe killed her; that she'd had a fallout with her head chef and he swore he'd kill her before he'd ever let her get away with what she did to him."

Alejandro never had gotten back to me. I wondered if he was working now.

"That must be the thing that happened with Jared. And he wasn't her head chef; he was the sous chef."

"Yes, that sounds more plausible than the story I heard, but no one knew why. After hearing the confirmation from you, that's what it had to be. The head chef has been here forever."

"Yes, he has."

Saylor nodded her head across the room as if she were pointing and I looked. "That's him. See, he wasn't fired."

I thought about walking over to talk to him, asking if he'd gotten my message, but we were there for the dinner shift, and even though he stood in the bar, he was probably working. I wouldn't want to be bothered in the middle of a shift, so I let it go. For the time being.

We spent the rest of the meal talking about Saylor's new real estate clients, and the other town gossip she's been privy to. Fully satiated with conversation and good food and wine, I got up and walked to Saylor's side of the table. I leaned in and kissed her on the cheek. "I'll pick up the tab next time."

She kissed my cheek, too. "Yeah, sure you will," she said with a huge grin.

"I will," I protested. "We'll eat at Savoie's."

With that, we both laughed a little too loud.

Saylor wiggled her brows and said, "I think I'm going to stay a bit longer, have another glass of wine, and maybe flirt with the chef."

I knew her well enough to know she had no interest in restaurant workers. They didn't have enough time for her. Saylor required high maintenance, but in a good way. I knew she was up to something. I hoped that meant snooping for me, but I didn't ask. I pretended I didn't want to know.

CHAPTER 15

Pierre arrived at the home before me, and unusual sight. At least I assumed he'd arrived home early, because his car was in the driveway. He may have been at the main house with Hettie.

I walked up to the back door and turned the knob, which was unlocked. Because of the amount of traffic on the property we lived on, we always locked our doors, even when we were home. I walked in, shut the door behind me and made sure it was locked before continuing into the house.

Oliver met me at the door, and I definitely took the time to give him scratches.

"What are you doing home?" I asked as I walked into the house.

Pierre stood in the kitchen. I didn't notice the earbuds in his ears until he looked up at me and pulled them out. No wonder he didn't answer me.

"Hey, where've you been? I stopped by your studio when I got home and you weren't there, so I assumed you were home." He seemed worried. "Oliver looked lonely, so I brought him home."

"I was at the Poached Pear with Saylor. We had a glass of wine and an appetizer. I guess you didn't hear me when I asked why you are home." I dropped my purse on the dining room table and stood with my hand on one of the chairs.

Pierre turned around to face me, leaning against the kitchen counter. "Gustav needed a different night off this week, so we traded."

"Really? What night?" There were certain nights guests expected Pierre to be in the kitchen and this concerned me. If they asked for him and he wasn't there, he'd better have a good reason. Switching shifts with one of his employees wasn't a good excuse as far as his patrons were concerned. I shook the thought out of my head. Not my circus anymore.

"It's not a big deal. He wanted Monday off." Pierre turned back to the skillet he had on the stove.

"That smells good. What are you making?" I inhaled deeply to savor the aroma.

"You're going to laugh," Pierre said. He took a taste from the spatula. "I'm trying one of your recipes."

I smiled. Pierre never tried other people's recipes because he was too busy making his own. "What is it?"

"It's your chicken risotto. I'm making it a little different than the recipe from your blog," he grimaced, waiting for me to chastise him for not trusting my recipe.

"You read my blog?" I couldn't keep the astonishment from my voice. Someone as successful as Pierre reading my little blog! I almost blushed.

"Of course I read your blog. I love that you have quick home recipes for people to make in their own kitchens. And the concentration on southern foods. I get so sick of seeing these blogs that try to mimic gourmet meals. Very few people can pull off what big kitchens do. I don't think they understand the amount of prep involved. And then they gum up the recipe by trying to make a homemade version of it. I looked through your recipes and you don't do that." Pierre reached for a spoon and took another sample of his risotto.

"I'm flattered," I blushed. "The point behind my blog was to make good food fast. Recipes people could make if they wanted to do meal prep or just everyday eating. If I want that luscious of a meal, I'm going out to dinner. Probably your place." I laughed on that last sentence. "And I love to throw regional recipes in there."

"Are you hungry?"

Pierre ditched the spatula he'd sampled from and grabbed a fresh one to stir the risotto.

"Sure. I just had a small appetizer when I was with Saylor, so I could find room for risotto. Anything I can help you with?"

Pierre pointed to the kitchen counter. "Can you toss that salad for me? It's just baby spring greens and some pomegranate dressing from my mom's place. I didn't want anything fancy because I'm not that hungry. And if this risotto turns out, we'll have leftovers for a couple of days."

I walked into the kitchen, washed my hands at the sink, then grabbed a paper towel to wipe them dry. Pierre already had two large salad forks on the counter, so I dribbled several tablespoons of dressing onto the salad, then use the forks to toss it. "Remember who you live with here. There may not be leftovers for days."

"Especially if Celine comes home early," Pierre said.

My whole body stiffened. "What do you mean if Celine comes home early?"

"Nothing. Sometimes she comes home on Friday night instead of Saturday morning. What's the matter with you?"

I picked up the bowl of salad and moved it to the dining room table. "I just wish she'd stay at school this weekend. I don't want her knowing anything about what happened to Annabel."

Pierre had grabbed a large serving spoon and dished out servings of the chicken risotto in small white bowls. "Parmesan?"

"Please."

"Celine's not five years old anymore, Marcy. She's wise to the ways of the world. We already talked about this. Someday, she's going to realize death happens to the people she knows, too. Sometimes death by murder."

"I know," I whined. "You know I'm not a helicopter parent. I was never one to hover. Heck, your mom hovered more than I did. But I just want to save her from this ugliness no one should have in their life."

"At least she wasn't the one to find Annabel. And I'm sure it wouldn't bother you as much if you hadn't been the one to find her. Celine will be just fine."

Pierre shoved large spoons into the bowls and brought them to the table. It was almost a repeat of the night before. Rarely did we sit down and have dinner together, and two nights in a row felt nice.

"You're right, finding Annabel has been on my mind nearly every minute."

"I wish we all could've been saved from this ugliness. I just can't imagine someone in our town that we know and who is so prominent, could be murdered." He took a deep breath at the end of his long sentence.

I scooped up a spoonful of the chicken risotto, and blew on it to cool it just a bit. I tentatively put the spoonful in my mouth, not knowing exactly how it would taste. It wasn't even a second before my taste buds burst. I wanted to swirl the creamy flavors around in my mouth and not even chew. The delicious tang of lemon combined with the mushrooms, onions, and chicken in the risotto felt like comfort food. I looked up to see Pierre staring at me.

With my mouth still full of food, I said, "What?" I never talked with my mouth full unless it was just me and Pierre. We'd been together too long to worry about such niceties.

"Well?" His eyes wide with eagerness.

I gave him the courtesy of finishing my food and swallowing before answering. "Oh my gosh, I am a great recipe developer. I do have to say though, adding the lemon zest and lemon juice gave it more zing than when I originally made the recipe. You, my dear, are a genius."

Pierre beamed with a grin. "We make a pretty good team, don't we?"

I know he didn't mean anything by it, but his words caught me off guard. We *had* been a pretty good team until he ruined it. There are just some things I could not forgive, and infidelity was one of them. I knew Pierre had had a weak moment, and the affair meant nothing, but it happened and would always be between us. Heck, I don't even know if I could call it an affair. It was a drunken one-night stand. And we had been contemplating separation at the time. I think things might have turned out differently if I had found out from him first. The thing that hurt my heart so much was I found out from someone else. That someone else was the girl he'd slept with. I tried not to think about it anymore, but sometimes it bubbled up, especially when Pierre made observations about what a great team we were. What we had; we could never get back.

Pierre must have seen the melancholy on my face because he quickly changed the subject. "My mom said you stopped by for lunch today. She said you were asking questions about Annabel's house."

I put my spoon down beside my bowl and wiped my face with a napkin. "I don't know why, but Annabel's murder is really bothering me. I dreamed about it last night. I just can't seem to let it go."

Pierre continued to eat. "You know we have a very capable sheriff's department, right?"

"Ha ha, I know. I just feel like maybe we know the family a little better than they do. Maybe we can find something that points in a different direction than where they're looking."

"Marcy, don't you have enough to worry about? Let the police do their job."

Suddenly, the risotto wasn't so tasty. I picked up my bowl and took it into the kitchen to dump the rest into a meal prep tray. "I told you; I can't get it out of my head. And I can't work if I can't concentrate. You know how it is. If your head is somewhere else, you don't cook as well. How am I supposed to develop recipes, photograph, and style them, and then write about them, when all I can think about is a dead person and who might have killed her?"

Pierre shoved another huge bite of the risotto into his mouth, then picked up his plate and walked into the kitchen. He stood next to me at the sink as I rinsed my bowl. He set his bowl down and touched me lightly on the shoulder. "I love you to the ends of the earth. If you feel the need to follow up and try to help the police, then you do that. But promise me one thing, that you'll be careful. And don't step on their toes."

Once again, he melted my heart. I leaned over and kissed him on the cheek. "I promise, I'll be careful. I can't promise about the toes though."

He put his bowl in the sink without washing it, then followed me into the living room. "Now we have that out of the way, I want to hear everything you've learned."

Pierre popped the cork on a deliciously sweet bottle of Moscato, and I told him everything I'd learned in my snooping, and about my new assistant.

CHAPTER 16

Once again, I didn't sleep well. The things running through my head made for nightmares. Annabel had come to talk to me, to tell me it was all a mistake. She wasn't really dead. Then Bobby Joe came to visit, covered in blood with a butcher knife in his hand. The only person who seemed to not be trying to tell me something was Jared. He just sat in the corner and smiled as the characters, some I knew and some I didn't, tried to explain Annabel's murder to me.

I awoke before the alarm went off and went directly to the kitchen to make coffee. I really wanted caffeine but forced myself to make decaf. Letting Oliver out, I went back to the bathroom to warm up the water for a shower.

A shower was exactly what I needed to try and clear my mind while the coffee brewed. Pouring black coffee over half-and-half, I added cinnamon flavored Stevia and twisted the lid closed on my travel mug. I carried the cup by the handle and walked out to my studio. I was ten minutes early and Jared was already there. I felt in my pocket for a hair tie so I could pull it up once it dried. Maybe I'd spent too long in the shower, because my fingers were wrinkly.

Oliver stood his ground on the sidewalk, hair straight up. He growled, but hadn't yet let out a bark. I walked up and said, "He's cool, Ol, you met him the other day."

Jared sat on the trunk of his car and when he saw me, he jumped down and walked with me to the studio. Oliver didn't seem so worried about him now, but Jared had the smarts not to try to pet him just yet.

"I'm sorry for all the trouble I've caused you. I'm so embarrassed." He had both hands shoved in the pockets of his chef's pants.

I waved him away with one hand, the one holding my coffee cup, as I put the key in the door with the other. "This isn't your fault." And then I looked back at him. "Unless you're actually the one who killed Annabel."

Jared's face lost all color. "Do you still think I killed her?"

I wanted to tell him I didn't think he killed her, but I also wasn't absolutely sure he didn't. I just didn't know. I chose not to respond.

Letting Oliver in first, I put my keys in my pocket while Jared went to the sink to wash his hands. This was ingrained in him after years of working in a kitchen.

Since I'd awoken that morning, I'd been contemplating the best way to get ahold of Jared's phone. I'd also been saying silent prayers that it wasn't password protected. Finally, as I walked to the studio, an idea came to me.

"We're going to try something new today. We'll do all the chopping and prep for this recipe in advance, because we're going to try making a video."

Jared dried his hands on a paper towel, then pushed the handle on the antibacterial dispenser and was rubbing it around on his hands. "Video?"

"Yes, all the bigger food blogs are doing videos now, thanks to Buzzfeed's Tasty and that darned TikTok. The one-minute recipe videos are all the rage. I haven't had the guts to try it yet, but I thought it might be fun. We'll make sure we have enough ingredients to make the recipe at least twice. Today, we'll prep two times what we need and split it. That way, if we have to re-film, we can start from scratch."

Jared's smile told me this was something he thought would be fun. "Who's going to be behind the camera?"

"You'll be on camera. Sorry to say, they won't see your lovely face, just your hands."

Jared held up his hands and flipped them back and forth. "If I'd have known that I would have gotten a manicure yesterday."

We both laughed. His hands looked fine. And besides, I had ulterior motives with this video idea. I didn't think it would ever end up on the blog.

"So, we'll chop and prepare everything, and have it premeasured in bowls. I think most people who read my blog already know how to chop onions, and smash and mince garlic. Or at least we're going to assume."

Eagerly, Jared grabbed an apron from the wall and put it on, tying it around his waist.

"Do you have your phone on you?" I asked.

Jared nodded and pulled it from his pocket.

"Put it on silent and place it on the other side of the room. I don't want you getting texts or calls in the middle of filming."

"Sure, I understand that. You want me just to turn it off?"

I hadn't thought it through, but said, "Just turning it on silent should be enough. If it vibrates, it'll be across the room, so it shouldn't interfere with anything. Besides, I think that's a sound that I should be able to remove in post if I needed."

For the next hour, Jared and I chopped, diced, and measured, and put everything in containers to be used for the video, making sure everything looked as pristine as I'd want it to be for a still photo. I did put my phone on airplane mode and propped it on the prep table. Just on case I wanted to use the video for real, and we'd have some prep video. While we did this, we discussed the best way to approach filming.

"How are you going to make it stand out from the rest?" Jared asked.

I wish I had an answer for him, but I didn't. "I don't know. That's something we'll have to come up with along the way." And then I thought to myself, *We'll just show Jared's face. The women will see him and the video will go viral.* He was so damn good-looking.

"Can I ask you a question, Jared?"

He looked at me but didn't say anything.

"What is a handsome guy like you doing with a married woman? You could have anyone you want."

He didn't answer right away, as if he was thinking about his answer. But the coloring on his face had a shade of green to it. "I don't know. Sometimes I just end up in situations."

This wasn't an answer, but I figured it wasn't my place to ask anyway. I let the subject drop. With the first set of ingredients, Jared and I did a run through with the video. As we filmed, I realized editing video was not going to be nearly as easy as editing a still photo. The learning curve on this one would be steep.

I'd been taking film school classes and editing courses online, and maybe I'd jumped the gun. It started off fun, and at worst, it was another wasted morning. But maybe not. It could be my best blog post to date.

We just finished filming the first round when I looked at my watch and realized lunchtime snuck up on us.

"I'm starving. How about you?" I asked.

"I figured you could hear my stomach growling during that last take."

I laughed. "Why don't you run up to the bed-and-breakfast and grab us lunch really quick? We can eat here." I looked at my watch again, almost one o'clock. No wonder his stomach was growling.

I hoped and prayed he'd forgotten his phone was on the table and not in his pocket and he'd take off for lunch without walking across the room to grab it.

"Do you want anything specific?" he asked.

"It's a chilly fall day, why don't we have soup? Unless you don't want soup."

"Soup it is. What kind?"

"Whatever Hettie has on the menu today. I'm not picky," I said.

"Sounds good. How about a loaf of French bread, too?"

Knowing Hettie's bistro made some of the best French bread around, I eagerly agreed.

Jared nearly ran out the door without even glancing toward his cell phone.

Just to be safe, I locked the door behind him.

As I walked over to his phone, I said a prayer to myself. *Please, no password, please.*

I picked it up and pressed the side button and swiped across the screen. Thank goodness, no password screen. I breathed a sigh of relief and got to work, thinking how trusting Jared was. Would a guy who had something to hide leave his phone unprotected? Well, I had nothing to hide, and I kept mine protected, so what did this say about me?

I went to the call log first and checked for Breanna's phone number. Unless Breanna had called me from a phone she didn't normally use to call him, she and Jared definitely didn't call one another often. I saw an outgoing call from his phone number to her the previous day. I pulled my phone out to check the timestamp on the incoming call. Jared had called Breanna's number nine minutes before she called me.

I scrolled back as far as five days and didn't see another phone call to or from the number Breanna used. I decided to check the text messages. There were several text messages that had timestamps after Breanna had called me.

The first from Jared: *Did you call her?*

Breanna: *Yes we talked.*

Jared: *Did you tell her we were together?*

Breanna: *Yes. I think she believed me.*

The last text was Jared thanking Breanna for making the phone call. I scrolled back through the phone, and the last time I saw anything from Breanna's phone number was something asking for a ride to work almost a month earlier.

That lying little turd. Now I wanted to get my hands on Breanna's phone and see what she had. Maybe this was a new phone number for her. But the text message saying that she thought I believed it sealed the deal for me. There was no way Jared was with Breanna that morning. And there was the fact she'd texted asking for a ride from that number.

When Jared came back from lunch, we wolfed down lunch, I feigned being jolly. I didn't want him to know what I knew. I sure didn't want my life in danger. The smart thing was just to play dumb. It was just the two of us in my studio, and the police would be at least fifteen minutes out if I still had any life left to call. I decided to pretend all was well and finish up the video shoot, then I'd go talk to John. I even contemplated ways to cut the day short, but I was so far behind on my work that I ended up keeping Jared until just before four.

I called the sheriff's department immediately after I saw Jared get in his car. John was out of the office, but they expected him back soon. I waited about ten minutes, to make sure Jared wasn't coming back, then got in my car and headed into town. I hoped and prayed John was in his office by the time I got there.

When I arrived at the sheriff's department, I stopped at the bullet-proof glass and announced myself. I heard a buzz on the other side of the door and it opened. Sheriff Waters, I mean John, met me on the other side.

"What brings you here?" John asked.

"I need to talk to you about some things. About Annabel's murder."

John looked like he wanted to roll his eyes, but he refrained and said, "Follow me."

I followed him into his office.

John sat at his desk and put his hand out to indicate that I should sit, too. I sat down and leaned forward with my elbows on his desk.

"We're working hard on Annabel's murder. We have a few leads, but I can't share anything with you," he said.

"But I can share some things with you." I put my hands flat on his desk. "Did you know that she fired her sous chef, Jared Guidry? That she accused him of stealing from her and promised to ruin his career? Telling him he'd never work in the East Texas again?"

"Like not working in East Texas is a big deal."

"I know it's not Dallas, but still, we have some amazing restaurants here."

"Fine, but yes, I knew."

This surprised me. "Who told you?"

"I talked to Patty Sue. She wanted to be sure that you understood you had a murderer working for you," he said, matter-of-factly.

I smirked. "I don't know about that. I think I'm a better judge of character than she's giving me credit for. But I am questioning myself, I guess." I paused. "Did I just contradict myself? Never mind, don't answer that."

"Whatever you say," he replied. He wasn't giving anything away.

"Well, your evidence must not be very solid, because you haven't arrested him yet. Does this mean there are other suspects?"

"You've been watching too many cop shows on TV."

I ignored his comment. "And did you know that Annabel and Bobby Joe had filed for divorce?"

I was so excited to be offering him this news.

"Yes, Bobby Joe told me this morning. He came in and we had a long chat." He sounded bored.

He sure was letting the air out of my souffle.

"Did you know that Jared's alibi is a fake?"

He leaned forward and said, "I didn't know Jared had an alibi. But I'm sure he does."

"He told me that he had fallen asleep in his car while listening to music. That he had been early for work, but then ended up being late because he fell asleep."

John leaned back in his chair. "That's what he told me, too, but that's not really an alibi."

I slapped my hand on the desk; I was so excited. John jumped. "He changed his story. He told me he was with Breanna Toomey from the Poached Pear. He claimed that they had been dating, and he had kept it a secret because Breanna was married."

John's eyes wide wide. He moved a yellow legal pad to the middle of his desk and picked up a pen. He wrote something quickly. "I hadn't heard about this yet. I'll have to investigate it."

"But there's more," I added. "I looked at Jared's phone. There's only one phone call and a handful of text messages between Jared and Breanna."

"What do you mean?"

"Breanna called me. Jared wasn't the one who told me that he was with her; she did. I had Breanna's phone number from the phone call, so I checked it against Jared's phone. For two people who are supposedly dating, they don't talk or text much."

John rocked forward in his chair, leaning in close. "And how did you get your hands on Jared's phone?" He didn't seem happy.

"He left it on the table in my studio, so I looked through it. There were a few texts that indicated he had asked Breanna to call me, and then Breanna said she thought I believed the story."

John shook his head. "You realize his call and text log could've been deleted. And you have no idea if the text messages were in context with Breanna calling you. Unless your name was mentioned."

I was getting flustered, and I could feel my ears turning red. The heat flushed all the way up my neck to my face. I couldn't believe he was blowing me off. "The only phone call to Breanna's phone was nine minutes before she called me. Then afterward, there were a few text messages and she said that she thought I believed it. And she's supposedly married."

"All the more reason to delete the call log. She wouldn't want her husband finding out."

"But it was Jared's phone. Not like he'd ever see Jared's phone," I protested. I hated that he was questioning everything I told him as if I was a crazy woman.

"Was your name specifically mentioned?"

I had to think for a minute. "No," I admitted.

"Like I said, the call log could've been deleted. And you don't know the exchange had anything to do with you. But I'll investigate it."

I got up to leave John's office, then turned around and said, "Oh, and I think there was something holding open the front gate at Annabel's house yesterday. I don't know for sure, but it had to be a boulder or brick or something. This morning, it was gone."

John stood and walked me out of the office. "Yes, we have it in our possession. I will tell you this, it wasn't a boulder. It was a piece of rope. The gate had been tied to a stake in the grass."

"What's the point of a security gate if you're not going to keep it closed?" I asked.

"We're looking into it. But the stake looked like it was placed for the purpose of keeping the gate open, and it's been there many moons," John said.

"The gate could've been broken. Did you ask Bobby Joe about it?"

As John walked me out of the building, he said he'd talk to Bobby Joe about it later.

I wanted to ask him if he'd looked into Bobby Joe having a life insurance policy on Annabel, but he seemed testy already. Maybe I'd ask Hettie. She'd know. And if not, maybe she'd ask John while they were recovering from their sexual antics. I cringed at the thought of Hettie in bed with anyone, much less the local sheriff.

I shivered as I got into my car.

CHAPTER 17

O n the way home from John's office, I couldn't help but swing by the Ryder building. I just wanted to see who was there, and to find out if Bobby Joe had taken the day off or if he was at the house. I thought maybe if he was at the office, I'd sneak back to the house one more time.

Pierre's admonishment to be careful chimed in my ears. Maybe going to the house wasn't such a good idea. Besides, I hadn't seen much of the house in recent years, and it probably wouldn't tell me anything the cops didn't already know. Wait, hadn't someone already said this to me? Heck, it was all jumbled, and I couldn't remember if I just thought it, said it, or someone said it to me.

As I drove slowly up to the intersection, stopping at the red light, I saw a familiar face.

A beautiful curvy blonde with a pixie haircut laughed as she walked out the door of Bobby Joe's building. She looked familiar, and it took me less than a second to register that this was Breanna.

I knew, other than charity work, that Bobby Joe's business and Annabel's businesses didn't cross. They were completely separate entities. Separate operations even. So what was Breanna doing at Bobby Joe's office?

Didn't she say she was up for promotion? And maybe now that Annabel was gone, Bobby Joe was taking over some of the management of Annabel's properties. This seemed plausible.

Breanna had hopped in her convertible Mercedes-Benz and motored down the road before my light turned green and I was able to turn into the Ryder parking lot. She must be a pretty good server to be driving a Mercedes. Then again, I didn't look closely enough to see if it was newer. An older Mercedes wasn't that spendy, other than the maintenance bill. Damn, I'd wanted to confront her. I considered following her, but common sense took over and I didn't.

As I walked into the office, Patty Sue looked up at me warily.

"Is something wrong?" she asked.

I cocked my head and frowned at her. "Wrong?"

"I haven't seen you this many times in ten years," she said with a genuine laugh. "And now this is the third time in as many days. I just assumed something was wrong." Patty Sue had her charm meter cranked up to eleven. Funny how her attitude changed when Bobby Joe was in the office.

I thought about the relationship between Patty Sue and Bobby Joe. She'd been his personal assistant for many years, and she knew things about the Ryder family most people probably couldn't even imagine. Not that she was supposed to know these things, but that's what happens when you're a personal assistant: you know things that other people don't. Part of the hefty salary was to pay the assistant to keep their mouth shut. I thought about offering to take her out for a glass of wine, but that would be insincere, and I couldn't pay her enough to betray her beloved Bobby Joe.

"That girl that just left here, she looks familiar, but I can't place her." I tried playing dumb to see what Patty Sue would tell me.

"Yes, that's Breanna Toomey. She works for Annabel. I mean, *worked* for Annabel." Patty Sue suddenly made herself busy.

"If she worked for Annabel, what's she doing here?" I knew the question was inappropriate almost as the words left my mouth.

Patty Sue looked up at me with raised brows and a look that told me she had no intention of answering my question.

"I saw Bobby Joe's car is here. I wanted to talk to him for a minute." I headed straight toward Bobby Joe's office.

Patty Sue jumped up from her desk. "No, you can't. He's busy. He's got a lot of catching up to do, and he's not exactly in the mood to work, considering his personal circumstances. He can't be bothered."

By now, she was standing in front of the door. I reached my hand around her waist, grabbed the doorknob and promptly opened the door to Bobby Joe's office.

I ignored Patty Sue completely, looking past her to say, "Hi, Bobby Joe."

Bobby Joe, who looked busy at his desk, glanced up and said, "Can I help you?"

The indifference in his voice made me think he didn't know who I was. But I knew this was impossible. Was he acting as if he didn't know me because of Patty Sue? None of it made sense.

"I just need a minute of your time. Can we talk?"

Bobby Joe looked at Patty Sue and nodded his head slightly. She stepped out of my way, and I waltzed into his office.

I moved to have a seat at his desk, then noticed a dark brown Louis Vuitton shoulder bag in the chair. I hesitated.

"Oh, sorry about that. Just throw it on the floor. I was planning to go to the gym after work. Lots of stress to work out of my system." Bobby Joe put his pen down and slid the papers he was working on off to the side. "What do you want to talk to me about?"

Now that Patty Sue was no longer between us, or in the room, he was much more cordial.

"I was just wondering how it went at the police station. Did you get everything worked out with the cops?"

Bobby Joe leaned back in his chair and let out a long sigh. "I think it went okay. I came clean and told him about the relationship problems Annabel and I had been having. I told him about the divorce, too, and answered any questions they had. I don't think I'm a suspect any longer." There was a palpable change in his tone. It sounded like relief.

"Have you learned anything new?" I was pushing my limits. I'd known these people for years, but we weren't *that* close.

"They haven't shared anything with me. Have you heard anything?" Bobby Joe asked.

I chewed on my bottom lip, wondering how much I should share with him. Then I decided he deserved to know, at least some of it. "Do you know much about the business doings at the Poached Pear?"

Bobby Joe looked at me and frowned.

"I'm trying to decide where to start. So, I'll just start. I hired one of Annabel's former employees. He didn't have the Poached Pear as one of his references, so I had no idea that he had worked at Annabel's restaurant. Patty Sue informed me that Jared Guidry, he's the guy I hired, had been fired from the restaurant. She told me he'd been stealing money and Annabel really read him the riot act."

Bobby Joe's lips all but disappeared before he said, "Yes, I know all about that. It was not a proud time for us, or for Annabel. She's--was still embarrassed she lost her temper the way she did."

"But that didn't stop her from blackballing Jared." I couldn't help but be a little defensive of Jared, even if I wasn't sure I trusted him. After all, where was the evidence?

Bobby Joe shrugged. "You know Annabel. She holds a grudge. I'm not surprised she blackballed him. But in reality, I think Annabel had bigger fish to fry."

"Jared was late to work the day Annabel died. And you know the cops say they're pretty sure Annabel was attacked and killed that morning."

"Where are you going with this?" Bobby Joe leaned forward, his elbows on the desk and his fingers steepled.

"Patty Sue made me think Jared could possibly have a motive for murdering Annabel, and when I asked him about his alibi, he said he didn't have one. Then suddenly I got a phone call, and he has an alibi. He said he was with one of the servers from the Poached Pear. They've been seeing each other and had been together that morning." I was saying it all wrong. "I mean, Jared didn't tell me he was with her; the girl called me. She explained that he didn't want to tell me because she's married, and he didn't want her to be involved because her husband was volatile." I looked toward the door and looked back. "And I just saw that same girl leaving your office. Breanna Toomey."

Bobby Joe chuckled. "Oh goodness, I promise you, Jared was not with Breanna the morning Annabel died. Nor is Breanna married."

I wasn't sure what was so funny. "And how do you know this?"

Bobby Joe dropped his hands on the desk. "Because I've been having an affair with Breanna for at least three months. We were in San Francisco. If you don't believe me, you can call or have the police check the video at the South San Francisco Hyatt Regency."

Almost to myself, I said, "So no quiet time at the cabin?"

He didn't respond.

I'm pretty sure my heart stopped. I should've left sleeping dogs lie. This was something I didn't want to know. So, Bobby Joe had been cheating on Annabel. And damn, now Jared didn't have an alibi again. But Bobby Joe sure did.

"For the love of God, Bobby Joe, you were cheating on Annabel?"

He put both hands up to stop me. "No, no, no. You don't understand. Annabel and I have been legally separated for over a year. She had every right to date, and so did I. Just because we were living in the same house didn't mean we weren't free to date other people."

That hit a little close to home. I wasn't sure I was ready for the day that Pierre started dating again. I think if that happened, one of us would have to move out. Considering it was Hettie's property we lived on, I'd be the one moving out.

I took a deep breath, trying to squash my anger. "You were with Breanna the morning Annabel died. That means that Jared doesn't have an alibi. Why on earth would Breanna call me?"

Bobby Joe shook his head. "I have no idea, but you can bet I'll be asking her. I do know this, she and Jared do not now, nor have they ever had a relationship. If they had, she would have been defending him to the end of the earth when Annabel fired him. That's just her personality. And maybe this was her way of defending him. Maybe he didn't steal that money."

Bobby Joe had a point. What if Annabel had discovered who had really stolen the money? Would she have confronted that person, too? Maybe she'd asked them over to the house to talk about it in private. If she was embarrassed about her outburst in public, maybe she thought it was a better way to take care of it.

"Did Annabel ever say she suspected someone else of stealing the money, other than Jared?"

"After a couple of weeks, she did admit that she was wrong about Jared. But she wasn't about to eat crow and admit it to anyone but me. It's funny, we still talked about a lot of business and personal things. We were still good friends. We just moved in different directions." His voice sounded far off, as if he was recalling a memory. "She did say she suspected someone else. But for the life of me, I cannot remember who it was."

I jumped up and nearly tripped over Bobby Joe's gym bag. "Oh my gosh, this is something else John needs to know. There's another suspect that the police aren't even looking into. This is huge, Bobby Joe, *huge*."

I went to the door and opened it, eager to talk to John and give him the information.

"I'm glad I could be of help. Do you want me to call the police?" Bobby Joe asked. He came around the desk, picked up his gym bag, and swung it over his shoulder.

"No, I need to talk to John anyway, so I'll let him know. Enjoy your time at the gym." I rushed past Patty Sue's desk but didn't see her.

CHAPTER 18

The door to the building had been locked. I had to wait for Bobby Joe to unlock it, then I followed him out. He locked the door behind us and set the alarm. "Marcy, thank you for your interest in finding Annabel's killer, but I do think you should stay out of it. Things could get dangerous, and I wouldn't want to see you get hurt."

Bobby Joe walked me to my car, and I wondered if his comment to stay out of it was a friendly warning or a threat.

"I'm just going to give John this one last piece of information, and then I think I'm done. I think this new direction will be the right one for the police. Thank you for your concern, Bobby Joe. Have a great night."

It was dark outside when I got out to my car, and I noticed that mine and Bobby Joe's car were the only ones in the lot. As I turned the key, I wondered: did Jared beat the other thief to the punch? I mean, he had been blackballed by Annabel. The rest was just speculation. If he was innocent, why would he have Breanna lie for him? Even if Annabel had been wrong, she'd still ruined him. What better reason to go after someone? She had completely stolen his livelihood and taken his career away from him.

I pulled out of the parking lot to head back toward the sheriff's office to tell him about this possible new suspect. When I arrived at the sheriff's office, I didn't see his car there. I drove into the parking lot anyway and parked, wondering if I should go in. Instead, I pulled out my cell phone and called the non-emergency number. The dispatcher who answered the phone told me that John was gone for the day, but I could leave a message if I wanted to.

"May I have his cell phone number, please?" I wasn't sure what had come over me. I mean, why would they give me the sheriff's cell phone number?

Nonplussed, the dispatcher said, "I'm sorry, we don't give out that kind of personal information."

Feeling stupid, I hung up without leaving a message. I'd go home and find out his number from Hettie. We all knew she had his personal information. I smiled to myself.

I hated driving after dark because my vision made headlights glare to the point of distraction. The glare bounced off everything, and I saw things in the road that weren't there. I'd been meaning to make an appointment with my optometrist. I'd even swerved a time or two to avoid hitting something that didn't exist. And for a second, I thought it was my imagination, but the car behind me seemed to be driving too close.

I considered slowing down to let them pass, but continued at my regular rate of speed. The car swerved and caught my rear bumper. I gripped the steering wheel to keep from losing control. Maybe slowing down to let them pass wasn't such a bad idea, so I took my foot off the gas. This didn't help the situation, because this time, the car behind me deliberately smacked into the backside of my car. Not a direct hit, but it slammed into the left side of my back bumper. My heart jumped into my throat. I didn't have a tight enough grip on the steering wheel and lost control. My car spun around, and I ended up with the nose of my car facing the opposite direction I'd been driving, and in the ditch. I looked to see what kind of car had crashed into me. The glimpse I caught looked like a late model black sedan. Dark colored car anyway, it wasn't easy to see.

As I was trying to maneuver my car out of the ditch and wondering how I was going to explain it to Pierre, my mind started reeling. Then it all started coming together.

The gym bag I had just seen in Bobby Joe's office was a Louis Vuitton brown canvas and leather bag. The one I'd seen in his office the day before had been an old, ragged, blue canvas bag.

I let this roll around in my head as I eventually drove out of the ditch (it wasn't a deep ditch), turned the car around, and headed home. I turned off the radio to listen to my car and see if there were any noises that shouldn't have been there. I heard a little rattle, but nothing that would keep me from getting home.

When I arrived on the property, I saw the sheriff's car. I blew out a breath of relief. John was at Hettie's house.

I drove up to the big house. John and Hettie were sitting on the front porch. I parked my car, got out, and walked around it to assess the damage. It looked like only the back bumper had been damaged from careening into the ditch, but the left back bumper was crushed. *Note to self, a Lexus will lose a fight with a late model sedan.* My entire body was shaking as I walked up to John and Hettie.

Hettie jumped from her rocking chair and jogged toward me. "My dear, are you okay?"

I looked at her with a quizzical look on my face. "What do you mean?"

John walked up behind Hettie and echoed her words. "Seriously, Marcy, are you okay? You look really shaken up."

I had no idea I looked as bad as my insides felt. Tears rolled down my cheeks as I said, "Someone just ran me off the road. I think they were trying to kill me."

Hettie wrapped her arms around me and hugged me tightly. "Oh, Marcy, I'm so sorry. I'm glad you're okay."

John looked at the two of us, not sure what to make of what I had said. I could see the questioning look on his face.

Hettie let me go and stepped back but stood close. "Start from the beginning, honey, and tell us what happened." She took me by the hand and walked me up the stairs, then made me sit in her rocking chair and stood beside me.

"I was at the Ryder building talking to Bobby Joe, when I had a revelation, so I thought I would go to the sheriff's office to talk to John. But he wasn't there, so I decided to come home and get his cell number from you, Hettie. Bobby Joe and I figured out that there might be another suspect. I wanted to let you know, so you could investigate."

John sat down in the rocking chair next to me. "Tell me what you learned. I'm not sure I don't already know, but I'm willing to listen."

And then before I could tell him about the possibility of there being another thief, I remembered the gym bags. "But then something else happened on the way home. As I was trying to figure out how I was going to get my car out of the ditch without calling a tow truck, Bobby Joe's gym bag flashed through my head."

Hettie asked, "What does Bobby Joe's gym bag have to do with anything?"

I looked at her. "The other day, when I went to go get the check for you, I opened the door to Bobby Joe's office. There was a blue canvas gym bag on the floor behind the door. It kept me from opening the door all the way. I assumed it was Bobby Joe's gym bag and didn't even think twice about it. It was a ragged blue canvas bag. I should have realized sooner that Bobby Joe would never own a cheap canvas bag."

John leaned toward me now. "Go on."

"Then tonight, when I stopped by to talk to Bobby Joe about my new assistant and find out what he knew, I saw a bag on the chair in his office. This bag was a Louis Vuitton canvas bag with a leather shoulder strap. It even had Bobby Joe's initials embossed on it. He told me to put it on the floor and said something about heading to the gym. So, if that was Bobby Joe's gym bag, what was that other bag?"

John asked, "Was that bag still in the office?"

"The brown bag, yes. Like I said, it was sitting on the chair in his office, and I moved it so I could sit down. But Bobby Joe took it with him when we left the office."

John shook his head. "No, the blue bag. Did you see it in his office this time?"

I thought about it. "No, there was nothing on the floor when I went in tonight. And to tell you the truth, it didn't even dawn on me until that car ran me off the road."

Now John had his hand on my knee, but in a fatherly way. "Did you get a good look at this car?"

"I didn't, but it was a..." I closed my eyes and tried to remember. "a big car. Dark, like navy or black."

I jumped up out of the rocking chair when my phone vibrated in my pocket. I don't know why, but it scared the crap out of me. I pulled the phone from my pocket and looked at the screen. I didn't recognize the number.

I answered tentatively. "Hello."

"Marcy, it's Bobby Joe Ryder." I could hear he was out of breath, as if he'd been running or was excited.

"Are you okay?" I asked.

"Oh, yes, I'm fine. I'm on the elliptical machine," he explained. "While I was working out, I remembered who the other chef was. You know, the other person who could have possibly taken the money."

I guess working out was good for the memory, too. "Really?"

I waited for him to say Alejandra Luna, but instead he said, "I hate to even say this, because it's Patty Sue's husband, Billy Osborne. He's Annabel's other chef, who normally works days."

"Wow, that's weird," I said.

"I know, and I can't believe I'd forgotten. I never did say anything to Patty Sue, because Annabel wasn't absolutely sure. No stirring the hornet's nest, since Patty Sue is an amazing assistant. Anyway, I thought you'd want to know. Especially if you're going to talk to the sheriff."

"Thanks," I started to disconnect, then said, "By the way, do you own a blue canvas gym bag?"

He didn't even hesitate. "Nope. Why?"

"No reason. I have to go." I put my phone in my pocket and turned to leave.

Hettie grabbed me by my upper arm. "No, you don't. You're not going anywhere, especially in that car. We'll have it towed into town in the morning and checked from nose to tail before you drive it again. Heaven knows what could've happened to the alignment or the axles when you went into that ditch."

I smiled to myself. She still loved me. Either that or...no, I was going with she still loved me.

I had planned to drive into town and confront Billy to see what he knew. I didn't know where Patty Sue and Billy lived, but I did know where he worked. I was just hoping that he was working the night shift, or at least hadn't left for the day.

John got up and stood in front of me. "Who was that on the phone?"

I looked at my watch. "That was Bobby Joe. He said the other employee who'd been suspected of stealing was Patty Sue Osborne's husband, Billy. He's one of the other chefs at Poached Pear. And if Annabel suspected him, that would mean that not only would Billy be out of a job, but so would Patty Sue. Now there's your motive."

John put his arm around me, then said to Hettie, "Go back in the house. Please. I want you to stay here until you see me again. Do you understand?"

A fierceness came across Hettie's face. She wasn't used to being told what to do. Then the look softened, as if she understood. "Be careful," she said as she walked toward the house.

"Are you walking me back to my house?" I asked. "Because I think I deserve to be there when you talk to Billy."

Oh, boy, was I pushing it. But he wouldn't have even known about Billy if not for me. Had they even looked in that direction? I waited for him to reprimand me. But I still wanted him to walk me to my house if I wasn't going with him. Or he could drive me, even though it wasn't that far. Or even follow me in his car as I walked. I think I was nervous because my thoughts got all jumbled.

"Come on, let's go have a talk with Billy," John said reluctantly.

We walked down the pathway to the cars, and he opened the passenger door of his sheriff's vehicle. I got in and buckled up, feeling a bit nervous.

It wasn't code three, but we did speed at quite a rate with the lights flashing as John maneuvered through the winding roads like an Indy car driving expert.

When we arrived in the city limits of Pear, he flipped the blue lights off and we cruised up to the Osborne house.

As we walked up the driveway, John noticed Patty Sue's car. "Look here." He pointed to the damage on the front passenger side of Patty Sue's dark blue Buick 300.

"My my," I said, feeling slightly nauseous.

"I want you to stay in the car," he said.

Oh, hell no. I didn't come with him, just to sit in the car. I got out when he did.

"Damn you, can't you take orders?"

"I want to see what he says."

John sighed. "Then stay behind me. I have a bulletproof vest, you don't."

I wanted to remind him that Annabel wasn't killed with a gun, but who was I to argue? I stood a step behind him.

John forcefully rapped on the front door.

Billy Osborne whipped the door open, as if looking for a fight.

"How can I help you?" Billy asked. Then he looked past John at me. "Don't I know you?"

"Billy Osborne, I'm Sheriff John Waters and this is Marcy Savoie."

A look of recognition came across his face Billy's face. "Yeah, I thought you looked familiar."

"Is Patty Sue home?" John asked.

Billy shook his head. "She hasn't gotten home from work yet. She sent me a text to tell me she was going grocery shopping first."

"Isn't that her car?" I asked.

Billy stuttered but didn't have an answer. When I looked past him into the house, I saw the blue canvas gym bag sitting in plain sight on the floor.

I tapped John on the shoulder and tried to point at the bag using only my eyes.

"Mr. Osborne, do you mind if we come inside?"

"What's this all about?" Billy did *not* open the door to let us in.

"I just wanted to chat with you about your job at Poached Pear, and Patty Sue's job with Ryder Industries."

"What's there to tell? We've both worked for the Ryders for a very long time. They've been very good to us."

John stepped forward. "Just humor me. We won't be more than a couple of minutes."

More than a couple of minutes? I fully expected an arrest before we left. Wasn't John taking me seriously?

Billy finally opened the door and let us in. John didn't step much further than the entryway. I walked around him, knowing that I couldn't get in trouble like he could for just opening the canvas bag to see what was inside.

I went for the bag. Bending over, I reached down quickly and unzipped it.

Billy grabbed for me, but I sidestepped him. "What are you doing?"

I didn't answer him. I finished unzipping the bag and pulled out a gray hoodie and sweatpants. The image on the video flashed across my brain.

Billy grabbed me by my collar and yanked me back. "Stop digging through my wife's gym bag!"

I struggled to get free of Billy's grip, kicking at him and missing his leg by a mile. I gave up the fight and let go of the sweats. He finally let go of me once I was standing.

He hadn't hurt me, but John had his hand on his Taser and was ready to stop him. It was only a matter of seconds, but I wondered why John wasn't on top of him immediately.

John and I looked at each other. Then he asked Billy, "Tell me the truth. Where is Patty Sue?"

Before her name had slipped through John's lips, I heard the back door of the house open and close. John didn't hesitate. He barreled past Billy and sprinted through the house, pulling his gun as he went. I tried to follow him, but Billy jerked me back.

I turned to punch him in the gut, but thought better of it when I saw the look of murderous rage on his face. He grabbed me and wrapped his arm around my neck, pressing hard against my throat. I started seeing stars in my peripheral vision. Then he loosened his grip, and I could breath and see normally again.

I kept thinking of ways to get free. Thinking of what to say to get him to let me go.

"I should have known you were trouble when you were snooping around at the restaurant," Billy snarled.

Before I could even struggle to get loose, John walked in with Patty Sue in handcuffs. Patty Sue's head looked as if it was going to explode. She was furious. John was huffing and puffing, trying to catch his breath.

Billy screamed, "Let her go, or I'll break this lady's neck."

John smiled. "We both know that's not going to happen. I have backup on the way, and you'll just make both of your lives worse. Besides, Marcy didn't do anything. She just came with me to identify the car that ran her off the road. Just let her go." His voice was so calm it almost made me angry.

Patty Sue struggled in John's grasp and screamed, "Kill her. I'm telling you Billy, you kill her."

Something in Billy snapped, I felt it in his entire body relax when Patty Sue screamed at him. He loosened his grip and shoved me away. "We wouldn't be in this mess if it wasn't for you. I'm not going to kill her."

I scampered out of Billy's reach and moved to the front door. I wanted to be able to escape in a hurry in case Billy changed his mind.

If Patty Sue's head could have literally exploded, it would have. "Oh, no, you don't get to do this now, you coward."

Hearing sirens in the distance, I took a chance and reached for the gym bag again. I said, "There is no way this is Patty Sue's gym bag. Look at these clothes." I picked up the hoodie that looked like it would be too big on Billy. Patty Sue would have swum in it. "Did you look at the videos?"

John didn't acknowledge my question because Billy sprinted past him and Patty Sue, and made a beeline for the back door. The front door would have been closer and easier, but that's where the blue and red lights were shining, illuminating the entire room like a disco ball.

John left Patty Sue and turned to give chase. I'm pretty sure he said, "I hate running," as he disappeared out the back door.

Silly me, I should have been paying more attention to Patty Sue and not John. She came at me full force and used her upper body to knock me to the ground. "I should have gotten rid of you when I had the chance. Nosy little rich girl."

My stomach hurt so much where she'd hit me, and I couldn't catch my breath. I wanted to respond, but I couldn't even consider uttering a word or even a moan. That crazy woman knocked the wind out of me and as I looked at her, she was getting ready to headbutt me.

Before she made contact, she was jerked back. I looked up to see Deputy Carter had yanked her by her handcuffs. She screamed in agony as her shoulders were wrenched backward.

My breath came back to me, and I snickered. Served her right.

Carter asked, "Are you okay?"

I nodded my head and sat upright. I still didn't want to speak.

Carter escorted Patty Sue out of the house, and a City of Pear police officer came in the house and helped me to my feet.

"You okay to walk?" he asked.

I could talk now and was more than slightly embarrassed. "I'm fine, thank you."

As he walked me out to the front yard, I resolved to start running again, and maybe even go back to kickboxing. I felt like an old woman for the first time in my life. And I wasn't even that old.

When we got to the patrol car, I saw John picking Billy up off the ground. He'd been cuffed and looked like there'd been a real struggle.

John breathed hard as he said, "Billy Osborne, you are under arrest for the murder of Annabel Ryder..."

I knew what was in the gym bag was circumstantial evidence, but it was a start. The person in the hoodie was the last person to enter the house before me, and the last person to see Annabel alive.

"Take them to the jail. I'll meet you there in about an hour," John said to his deputy.

I sat in the front seat of John's car. Patty Sue rode in Carter's car, and Billy in the patrol officer's car.

John got in his car and said, "I'm taking you home. Unless you want to go see a doctor. Carter said Patty Sue hit you pretty hard."

I took a deep breath, and it didn't hurt, so I said, "Home it is. Thanks."

I slept better that night; no nightmares that I could remember, anyway. It might have had something to do with the glass of whisky I'd chugged while telling Pierre and Hettie about the night's events. Or maybe it was the third glass that did it.

John's car was at the house in the morning when I got up.

If I'd felt bad for Hettie when she was hungover, I felt for her even more now that I could physically relate. My back hurt from hitting the floor. My gut hurt from Patty Sue slamming into me. My head hurt because I was foolish enough to drink that third glass of whisky.

The sun had barely come up over the mountain when I hiked up to Hettie's house, stopping ever so often to dry heave into the grass.

John and Hettie sat on the back veranda, enjoying the sunrise and drinking coffee. He looked up and smiled at me. "You look like hell."

I forced a smile. "Gee, thanks."

Hettie turned to look at me. "Hangovers suck. Make yourself a cup of coffee." She pointed to the coffee table set up in the corner of the veranda.

I did just that and sat in the chair across from them, my back to the sun.

"Thank you for your keen sense of observation. You likely saved us some man hours trying to solve this murder." John raised his coffee mug in a gesture of camaraderie.

I shrugged. "I don't know how much help I was. I just found the clothes. Not much else."

John laughed. "Sometimes that's all you need. That and leverage."

I frowned. "What do you mean?"

"Remember how I'd told you that you've been watching too many cop shows? Well, this one could have been a scene from almost any of them."

Hettie asked, "Why do you say that?"

"We pitted Patty Sue and Billy against one another. Patty Sue caved first. She took a plea deal and even told us where to find the murder weapon." John grinned.

"What? Really?" I said in a high-pitched voice that even hurt my ears.

"Patty Sue was charged with conspiracy after the fact. Apparently, she was supposed to get rid of the gym bag by burning it, but she hadn't had the chance before we arrived at the house. She said Bobby Joe had her working overtime while he was out of town, and running in circles since he'd been preoccupied with the murder of his wife. She'd barely gotten the gym bag out of the office while you were there."

"I thought it was weird when she left the office yesterday before Bobby Joe did. She didn't even tell him she was leaving."

"That's why the bag was at the house. Why she didn't dump it sooner is beyond me. Oh, and the murder weapon was still in the Ryder house. It was a crystal bowl. It had been washed and put back in its place in the China hutch. We're having it tested for Annabel's blood, hoping it wasn't washed that thoroughly. We're also hoping for a chance of fingerprints, but the lab is doing that, not us. Now we're waiting for DNA results and other blood analysis."

Later, John had told me that there may have been blood on the bottom of the athletic shoes. That was being tested, too.

Billy had yet to say a word.

Epilogue

Time had passed, but I couldn't help myself. Even though I knew Bobby Joe had nothing to do with Hettie's murder, I stopped by his office to ask him about a life insurance policy.

He'd hired a new assistant, and she looked like an older version of Patty Sue.

He did, in fact, have a policy on Annabel's life, and she had had one on him.

"It was a business matter. If she died, we needed to be able to continue without her. The amount of the policy reflected that. And I'm not the beneficiary, my kids are. I figured they deserved something."

I didn't ask the amount, because that would be rude, and I knew the number would make my head swim.

"I'm glad you're looking out for the kids," I said.

"Actually, both my son and daughter are coming back to Pear. They'll be taking over the vineyard and winery. I'm happy to have them back in my life." Bobby Joe smiled.

"I thought the winery would be sold if Annabel died? And the proceeds were going to charity or something." Isn't that what he'd said?

"Yes, well, that would only happen after I died. And I hope to live long enough for my kids to be able to purchase the vineyards and winery with the life insurance money. I'll be investing it for them. Until then, they are taking over Annabel's position on the board of directors. I gave up my seat so both the kids would have equal positions."

"I didn't think you were involved with the grapes," I said, perplexed.

"Not hands on, but I've been a board member from the beginning. There's a lot of red tape, but I think the vineyards and winery will stay in the family."

"That's great," I said, and I meant it.

"Whatever happened with you and Jared?" he asked.

"I asked him why he lied. He said he was terrified because he didn't have an alibi. He really had fallen asleep in his car." I remembered the pallid hue to his skin as he told me the truth.

"And does he still work for you?" Bobby Joe asked, as if he had ulterior motives.

"Yes, and he's staying with me, so don't even think about it." I shook my finger at him.

Later that week, Hettie had a dinner catered by Savoie's and the four of us; Hettie, John, Pierre, and I enjoyed the evening. Before dinner, we sat in the formal living room, testing a new varietal from Savoie's winery and munching on hors d'oeuvres.

Pierre had become more curious than me after learning the identity of Annabel's killer. "I just don't get it. Why?"

John chuckled. "I can't tell you a whole lot, but I can tell you this: Patty Sue had been in love with Bobby Joe for years, but she knew it wasn't going to go anywhere, so she suffered through with Billy. In the end, I wonder if she was in love with Bobby Joe or his money, but that's beside the fact. Apparently, it was Patty Sue who'd come up with a plan to embezzle money from Annabel."

This was the first time I'd heard of this. I was intrigued.

"She went on a rampage once we got her in an investigation room. She went on and on about how she did everything for Bobby Joe, and that they'd even had a short affair before Breanna came along. She was sure Bobby Joe was going to pick her, and then he didn't. She had enough information about the Ryder's finances to take the money. She told Billy how they could get away with it, and how they could pin it on Jared. And when he got fired, they had to come up with a new scheme. That's when Annabel invited Billy to the house."

"It was just so weird that he didn't drive to the house and up the driveway," I said.

"I think he knew it wasn't going to end well, and he wasn't going to take the fall. But I don't think he'd planned to kill her." John stopped talking, then said, "If you ever repeat that, I'll deny I said it, because we're gunning for first degree murder, hoping he'll plead down and save us a trial."

"Birds of a feather..." Hettie said quietly.

I finish the sentence for her, "...flock together. And those two were birds of a feather for sure."

"They both had completely clean records. Not so much as a traffic ticket before all of this. Who'd have thunk it?" John, out of uniform for once, was enjoying his glass of wine.

"So, with the divorce coming, Patty Sue thought Bobby Joe would be free, and she would have her foot in the door?" I asked.

John said, "I think that's it. Then she realized Bobby Joe wasn't even remotely interested when he dumped her for Breanna; a newer, prettier, smarter model."

I put my hands up. "Whoa, there. Just because Breanna was younger, it doesn't mean she was prettier or smarter." I turned and glared at Pierre. This would never be over between us.

"Marcy's right. It could've just been a weak moment for Bobby Joe. One that he will now forever regret," Pierre said, then stuffed an appetizer in his mouth and walked away.

"I don't think Bobby Joe regrets Breanna one bit," Hettie said. "But he definitely regrets Patty Sue. Everybody knows that you don't poop where you eat. He should've stayed far, far away from her. If she never thought she might be able to get her hands on Bobby Joe's fortune by having an affair with him, then leaving Billy, she'd never have come up with the scheme to steal from the Ryders in the first place. Well, maybe not."

Swirling the wine in his glass, John said, "I agree. But greed does funny things to people. And when Billy and Patty Sue realized they'd been found out, and that Annabel would not only ruin them, she'd make sure that they were tried and convicted, they panicked."

"And knowing Annabel, she'd have paid off the judge to make sure they each got life sentences just for the embezzlement," I laughed.

Everyone laughed along with me, then we all got solemn, remembering someone was dead.

"No more morbid talk," Hettie said. "This is a celebration. A celebration of Annabel's life, and to finding her killer."

We all agreed.

Hettie raised her glass and said, "To Annabel."

If you enjoyed reading this novel, I would appreciate it if you would help others enjoy the book, too.

Lend it. This eBook is lending-enabled, so please feel free to share with a friend.

Recommend it. Please help other readers find the book by recommending it to readers' groups, discussion boards, Goodreads, etc.

Review it. Please tell others why you liked this book by reviewing it on the site where you purchased it, on the reader sites online, or on your blog.

Email me. Jamie@authorjamie.com

Recipes mentioned in the book

SUN-DRIED TOMATO BASIL PESTO

This pesto would pair nicely with a Petite Syrah or Chardonnay.

INGREDIENTS

1 cup oil-packed sun-dried tomatoes (drained)

1/2 cup grated Parmesan cheese

1/4 cup chopped fresh basil or 1 tablespoon dried

2 tablespoons slivered almonds, toasted (I prefer almonds to pine nuts because they are less expensive and easy to find at any grocery store)

3 garlic cloves, peeled

3/4 cup olive oil

PREPARATION

Add sun-dried tomatoes, Parmesan cheese, basil, slivered almonds and garlic to your food processor. Run your processor and slowly add olive oil until everything is combined into a smooth paste. This will keep in the refrigerator for at least 2 weeks in an airtight container.

When using the pesto on your pasta, reserve ½ cup of your cooking water and combine ¾ cup of pesto, add to drained pasta and toss over low heat to coat the pasta.

If you are cooking a single serving of pasta, reserve a tablespoon of the liquid and combine with a heaping tablespoon of pesto for each serving.

BASIC HOMEMADE PASTA DOUGH

INGREDIENTS

4 Cups All-Purpose Flour4 large Eggs

PREPARATION

Place the flour in a mound in the center of your work surface. I use a marble cutting board, but wood is great too. Make a well in the center of the flour and place cracked eggs into the well.

Using your clean hands, break the egg yolks and begin to incorporate into the flour, starting with only the middle and edges of the well, and working your way outward until you've incorporated all the flour into the eggs. Keep pushing everything toward the center to keep the shape. This step is messy.

Once the dough starts to hold together, start kneading, using the heels of your hands. Once you have a nice mound of dough, continue to knead for about 10 minutes. Dust your board with more flour as needed.

Once your dough is elastic and only a little sticky, portion into 4 separate balls and wrap in plastic wrap and give it a 30-minute nap.

MAKING YOUR NOODLES

Pasta Roller directions:

Flatten the dough on one end and feed into the pasta machine. Feed it all the way through with the **rollers on the largest setting. Once fed through, fold into thirds, and roll again.** Repeat this process, narrowing the roller settings as you go, until the dough is the desired thickness. **Roll slowly to avoid cracks.Fettuccine noodles: cut the sheets about every 12 inches.** Attach the fettuccine noodle cutter (it has approximately 1/4-inch slats) to the pasta machine and dust it with flour, spinning the roller to coat completely. Feed one end of the pasta sheet into the rollers, and out comes perfect fettuccine. Run the entire sheet through the cutters, then dust the noodles lightly with flour so they don't stick together. Roll into small nests if you will be storing the pasta. Otherwise, you can drop the noodles right into the water to cook.

Tip: If you're working with only a portion of the dough at a time, keep the remainder wrapped in plastic to prevent it from drying out. **No pasta machine? No worries.** Roll your pasta dough out flat, fold it into thirds, and roll flat again, repeat this about 3-5 times or as long as it takes for the pasta to develop a sheen.

To make noodles, cut the sheets for the length of noodle you prefer (6-12 inches), lightly roll the sheets into a log and using a sharp knife, cut the log at approximately every ¼ inch. Once all your noodles are cut, unroll them and lightly flour.

COOKING

Fresh pasta cooks much faster than store bought noodles! Small shapes can take less than a minute. Fettuccine might take five minutes.

STORAGE OF NOODLES AND PASTA BALLS

I roll my fettuccine into small nests, and lightly flour before putting it in the refrigerator.

You can store fresh pasta in the fridge for 3-5 days, or freeze for up to a month.

Fresh pasta is so much better than dried or frozen. Most important, make sure you keep the stored pasta away from moisture.

CUCUMBER AVOCADO SANDWICH WITH POME-GRANATE MAYO

Pinot Grigio or if you like bubbles Prosecco would be delightful with this sandwich.

Ingredients

4 slices of whole grain bread (toasted if you prefer)

1 large Cucumber

1 large Avocado

2 T Plain Greek Yogurt

¼ C Light Mayo (or regular for more yumminess)

3 T Pomegranate Vinaigrette

preparation

If you have a spiralizer, make spirals out of the entire cucumber. If you don't, then thinly slice the cucumber into 1/8 inch slices (approximately). Place in a medium sized bowl and toss the cucumbers with the plain Greek yogurt.

In a small bowl, whisk together the mayo and pomegranate vinaigrette until smooth and well blended.

Halve avocado and make ¼ inch slices in the meat while still in the skin. Scoop out with a tablespoon.

Spread pom-mayo on one slice of bread, then top with ½ of the yogurt covered cucumbers, layer with ½ of the avocados, then add a generous amount of the pom-mayo on the second slice and top the sandwich.

This is a delicious healthy sandwich and is a nice no-cook treat in the summer.

Makes 2 sandwiches.

PB&J AND BRIE SANDWICH

Totally yummy with a bubbly Moscato or Pinot Grigio, or a chilled blackberry wine.

Ingredients

4 piece of flatbread or 4 thick tortillas, 8 inches

2 T Peanut Butter (or more if you love peanut butter)

2 T favorite jelly (I prefer grape jam with this, but strawberry is delicious too)

½ Wheel of Baby Brie (3.5 oz.) you can add more cheese to taste.

1 T butter

preparation

Melt butter over medium heat in a medium skillet. Pre-toast the flatbread or tortilla by placing them in the oven or toaster.

Remove flatbread and let cool, about a minute. Spread 1 T peanut butter and 1 T jelly on 2 of the pieces of flatbread. Remove outer coating of Brie and cut into ¼ inch slices and divide evenly on the other 2 pieces of bread.

Place the bread with the Brie back in the skillet (cheese side up) until the cheese begins to melt (30 seconds to 1 minute usually) Once the cheese has started to melt, place the other slice of bread with the PB&J side down, over the cheese. Allow to warm for 15 seconds and remove from skillet to a plate.

Makes 2 sandwiches. Serve with lots of napkins because it's messy.